# AQUAMAN

## THE DELUXE JUNIOR NOVEL

# AQUAMAN

## THE DELUXE JUNIOR NOVEL

ADAPTED BY JIM McCANN

AQUAMAN CREATED BY
**PAUL NORRIS** AND
**MORT WEISINGER**

SCREENPLAY BY
**DAVID LESLIE
JOHNSON-McGOLDRICK**
AND **WILL BEALL**

**HARPER**
*An Imprint of HarperCollins Publishers*

HARP41450

Library of Congress Catalog Number: 2018952745
www.harpercollinschildrens.com
ISBN 978-0-06-288907-2 (trade bdg.)—ISBN 978-0-06-285225-0 (pbk.)
18  19  20  21  22    PC/LSCH    10  9  8  7  3  5  4  3  2  1
Book design by Erica De Chavez
❖
First Edition

# A Q U A M A N

## THE DELUXE JUNIOR NOVEL

*"Put two ships in the open sea, without wind or tide, and, at last, they will come together."*
—Jules Verne

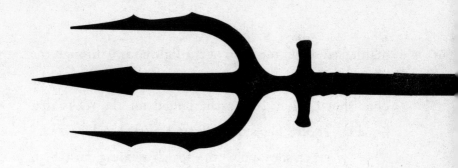

# PROLOGUE

**AMNESTY BAY, 1985**

The wind howled that night as though the sea were crying out like a wounded animal. The rain bore down in torrents. The dark sky flashed as lightning streaked across it in a rage. Through it all, the beacon from the lighthouse's watchtower illuminated the sea and sand as it swept back and forth, patrolling the surf.

From his perch in the gallery of the lighthouse, Tom Curry thought he saw something bobbing in the violent waves. Tom swept back his wavy brown hair and leaned over the rails to get a better view. Lightning lit the air, revealing something washed up on the rocks. The young man raced down the steps of the lighthouse, through the kitchen, and out the front door. The wind slammed the door shut behind Tom as he bolted for the rocks that lined the shore. The storm shutters rattled in his wake.

A wave crashed upon the rocks, sending mist high into the air. Tom wiped it out of his eyes and looked closer. He was right—there *was* something the waves had carried in on their tumultuous tide. Shielding his eyes from the downpour, he saw something that made him run to the rocks with renewed urgency—locks of golden hair lay across the rough terrain. The sea hadn't washed some*thing* ashore, but rather, some*one*. Someone who needed Tom's help. The lighthouse keeper hoisted the unresponsive woman into his arms.

Though she was helpless, unconscious, nothing about her seemed weak. Her clothing was completely foreign to Tom; it looked at first to be a wet suit, but looking closer, it seemed to be some kind of armor. Blood was seeping out of one of the tears. She was injured! As he turned to bring her back to the safety of his home, something sharp pricked his leg. In the woman's hand was a gleaming trident, the likes of which Tom had only read about in tales of sea mythology. The staff curved at the end, forming five sharp points. He tried taking it from her, but it was as though the trident were an extension of the woman's arm, so tight was her grip on it. He put the thought out of his mind, focused on the fact that the woman wasn't breathing. He had to act quickly.

Tom burst through the front door, shoved the table setting for one onto the floor, and laid the woman on the table. The door crashed, closed by the wind, as the television blared something about flash flood warnings from the unexpected high tides. The lighthouse keeper tuned all of that out, intently focused on getting the woman to breathe again. He began to perform CPR, pushing one, two, three, four, five times on her chest before blowing air into her mouth. Nothing. He tried again. Still no response. Lightning struck nearby outside, causing the lights and TV to go dark.

"Come on!" Tom took a deep breath and had moved to repeat the process when he was suddenly stopped. The woman's eyes had snapped open.

The emerald green in her eyes seared through him, as though she was about to lash out at an intruder. Her eyes widened in shock as she coughed, spitting out water and, to Tom, it seemed, choking on the air around them. Finally, she took a deep breath in.

"You—you're alive!" But Tom's joy disappeared as his

"damsel in distress" sprang off the table, spun around to face him, and pointed her trident at his face, poised to kill.

Tom raised his hands. "You weren't breathing," he managed to choke out, eyes on the deadly prongs of the trident.

At once, the lights snapped back on and the television again began loudly broadcasting the severe weather alerts. The woman twisted her wrist slightly and hurled the trident, impaling the TV. She turned back to glare at Tom. He knew he should be scared, but for some reason he felt something far different from fear. The way the woman moved was so fluid it was as if they were underwater. He admired her.

Just as he was searching for the right thing to say, the golden-haired siren who'd washed up on his shore, the killer of his television, collapsed into his arms, unconscious.

The next morning, the mystery woman stirred. She had slept the entire night on the couch without moving, a well-worn blanket wrapped around her. Tom looked over from the kitchen, where he was frying eggs. He poured two cups of tea from the kettle on the stove and walked over to her.

Tom blew on his mug. "Careful, it's hot."

She took the mug from his hand, looking into the

warm water. She brought it to her lips, blowing on it as well.

"That's right," Tom encouraged her and took a sip. The woman mimicked him, a look of surprise flashing over her face as she drank.

"I'm making some breakfast. I'm sure you're hungry after the night you had." Tom glanced across the cozy living room to the television, where her trident remained pierced in the now-defunct screen. "Um, just curious, but where did that come from?"

The woman looked at him a moment, then stood and retrieved her trident.

"Who *are* you?" Tom couldn't keep the curiosity from his voice anymore. He had stayed awake all night, running possible scenarios in his head as to the woman's origin.

She stood taller, cleared her voice, and finally spoke. "I am Atlanna, queen of Atlantis."

Of all the theories Tom had concocted, this was certainly not one of them. He moved to her, extending his hand to shake hers. Atlanna glanced at it and looked back into Tom's eyes, not returning the gesture.

"I-I'm Tom, uhhh, keeper of the lighthouse," he said, gesturing around his own small "kingdom."

He gave a nervous smile as he reached over and

picked up a snow globe. Inside was a replica of the lighthouse. Atlanna looked at it quizzically. Tom shook it, and Atlanna gave a look of wonder as tiny artificial snowflakes floated in the water, coating the lighthouse in a dusting of white. Tom's smile was genuine this time.

It was winter. Atlanna stood atop the lighthouse perch looking out to the sea as she had done daily in the months since Tom had rescued her. As Tom came out to wrap a blanket around her, he wondered if she was looking longingly at a home she missed, or keeping watch for something worse to emerge from the waters.

Tom had learned from Atlanna that she had fled her undersea kingdom to escape the unhappiness of an arranged marriage to a man she didn't love. In doing so, she had betrayed not only her ruler, but her entire kingdom. She hadn't known what to expect when she'd escaped the guards who had chased her that stormy night that she washed up on the shore. As snow began to fall around her, she reached out to catch a snowflake. *Every day seems to bring something new*, Tom thought, smiling. Something unexpected.

Looking into Atlanna's eyes, he saw the most unexpected surprise of all: love.

"Residents are advised to seek shelter inland as the Category Four hurricane Arthur is expected to make landfall within the hour . . ."

The local meteorologist was updating the situation, weather maps flashing across the new television set. It had been nearly a year to the day that the two lovers had first met, and, like that fateful night, a storm was raging once more. Atlanna smiled.

"We're safe here. I can read the tides." Her voice was as confident as ever.

Pulling her in closer, Tom put his arms around her pregnant belly. "What about naming him Arthur?"

"After the hurricane? I hope our son will be a bit calmer. Although the way he kicks, I feel like he's enjoying swimming around in here," Atlanna said, placing her hand on Tom's.

"After a legend. He is a king, after all." Tom held her, feeling their unborn child kick.

Atlanna looked out through the storm at the sea. "He's more than that. He is living proof that our people, those of the land and the sea, can coexist in harmony." Her voice was tinged with hope. "One day, he shall be the one to unite our two worlds."

Lightning struck and lit the night sky, giving Tom and Atlanna a clear view of the ocean's swelling waves. There was no thunder that followed, as though nature itself approved the peace Atlanna hoped their child could one day restore.

Arthur was chewing on a picture frame, as three-year-olds do. Tom stifled a chuckle as he took the wooden frame from his son's hands. He looked at the picture—it showed Atlanna leaning against him, their newborn son wrapped in the same blanket that had kept her warm the night she entered Tom's life.

"Yeah, this is one of my favorites, too, son," he said. "You know what else is a favorite of mine? Your mother's stories. Be a good boy and pay attention; you'll need to know all about both sides of where you came from one day."

Atlanna smiled as Arthur climbed back into her lap. She was holding a homemade doll wielding a mighty wooden fork in its hands. As she began Arthur's favorite story, Arthur clapped in delight.

"The Original Trident could only be wielded by the strongest Atlantean," she said, shaking the fork. "It gave King Atlan mastery over the Seven Seas. However, he became so powerful that the ocean itself grew jealous and sent a terrible earthquake to *destroy* Atlantis!"

Arthur covered his eyes, peeking through fingers that were already stronger than those of most children twice his age, as his mother's voice grew ominous. "Down, down, down Atlantis tumbled, crashing below the waves and deep into the sea. It cracked into seven pieces as it fell before settling on the ocean floor."

Arthur gasped. Atlanna took the fork from the doll and held it up. "Legend has it that one day a new king will rise to power. He will find the lost trident of Atlan and use it to restore the Seven Kingdoms into a unified Atlantis, bringing peace, unknown for centuries."

She handed the fork to Arthur, a symbol of his destiny. Arthur began to chew on the fork, giggling.

"I'm not sure which he likes more, the story or the fork," Tom said, laughing at their son's alternating actions of jabbing the fork in the air and chomping enthusiastically on it.

"He's destined for great things, Tom. I can feel it. One day, I hope to bring him to my people as a symbol of peace, and they will see that wars and fighting can . . ." Atlanna's voice trailed off as she looked past Tom and out the window, something in the sea suddenly capturing her attention.

Tom sensed a change in Atlanna even before she yelled

his name. At the sound of her warning, "TOM!" he ducked beside the couch and covered Arthur with his own body as the wall exploded inward from a powerful gush of water.

He turned to see a pair of strangely suited figures enter through the opening in the wall. Tom could only describe them as wearing what appeared to be high-tech deep-sea-diving suits—skintight, showing bodies toned for fighting; helmets with water *inside* them, the faces inside clearly breathing the seawater; and carrying strange blasters that fired water like a cannon.

"Hydro-pulse rifles!" Atlanna shouted. With a swiftness he had only seen once before—on the night they met—Tom watched Atlanna streak across the room and kick the nearest soldier hard in the ribs. Atlanna had been injured the night they met, so Tom had only witnessed a fraction of his love's capabilities. Now, as she fought to defend Tom and Arthur, he saw just how strong and deadly Atlanna was. He understood why she was a queen.

A blast of water erupted from the rifle of the other soldier, nearly hitting Tom. Atlanna leapt in a fluid motion and, with deadly precision, spun in midair and kicked through the glass of the soldier's helmet, leaving him unable to breathe. Two more soldiers stormed in through the hole in the wall. Looking up, Tom saw Atlanna's trident mounted on the wall where they had hung it years ago.

"Atlanna!" Tom threw the trident to her. The two operated like one as she reached up and caught her weapon without looking back.

"RRRRAAAGHHH!" Atlanna's fury was unleashed fully as she knocked back the two advancing soldiers that remained with a single thrust.

Without taking time to catch her breath, she scooped up the soldiers, two under each arm. Running to the pier, she threw their bodies back into the sea. As she returned, her eyes were beginning to swell with tears.

"It's okay. You were amazing. We're safe now." But Tom's assurance was met with resistance as Atlanna shook her head. These weren't tears of relief, he realized. As he searched her eyes, he knew what this was: goodbye.

She walked across the room, hung the trident on the wall, and looked at her son. This would be all he would have of her, aside from stories and pictures. Tom picked up Arthur and joined Atlanna as she walked to the edge of the pier.

"You don't have to do this, Atlanna." Tom's voice cracked as he pleaded his case. "We can run. Away from the ocean, far into the mountains, or to a city where they—"

Atlanna's hand on his arm told him this was one

decision that was out of either of their hands. "They'll come back. They know I'm still alive, and no matter how far I go, they will be relentless." She stroked her toddler's curly hair. "You must look out for our son. Please tell him I did this for him. For all of us."

"He'll ask about you," Tom said. They both knew their son would never stop wondering where his mother had gone.

She wiped a tear away from Tom's eye and used the same finger to wipe away one from her own. She pointed to the pier's edge. "One day, when it is safe, I'll return to you. To both of you. Right here, at sunrise, we will meet again, I swear. And it will be forever." She choked back more tears.

"Forever." Tom tried to sound hopeful.

Giving the two most important people in her life one last kiss, she turned and dived into the sea, deep down to the land that she had told stories of, the kingdom that demanded its queen's return.

Tom stood for almost an hour, Arthur by his side, holding his hand. He looked out to the ocean and made his own vow—he would wait at sunrise every morning for his love to return. Giving a final glance, he scooped Arthur into his arms and carried the young child back up the pier.

Arthur was looking at the sea again—rather, a tiny fraction of it, encased in glass. The glass went from the floor and arced over his head and back down to the other side, forming a tunnel of sea life surrounding him. He was on a field trip to the aquarium.

It had been six years since his mother had left. Six long years of watching his father greet the sunrise at the end of the pier every morning, only to return alone. Six years of stories of a fantastical kingdom in the ocean's depths, where his mother had returned to rule until one day she could be free and rejoin her family. Six years of wondering whether to believe the stories.

As Arthur looked at the seawater behind the glass and the ocean life that filled it, a part of him sensed he wasn't normal. Especially here. Even through the glass, Arthur could taste the brine, smell the tang of salt, and, if he quieted his own thoughts, almost feel . . . *something*. His father told Arthur it was the song of the sea, but he didn't know what that meant. Whatever it was, there was definitely something more to it.

"All life came from the seas," the tour guide's voice droned, repeating the same speech he had given dozens of times to hundreds of guests. "So if we want to understand ourselves, we must journey to where we began."

"Hey! Can they hear us?" Mike, a pathetically dim classmate of Arthur's, pounded on the glass.

"Yeah," chimed in Matt, Tweedledee to Mike's Tweedledum, also banging.

Arthur's strange feeling grew as the boys hit the glass harder and harder. He turned back to the glass and saw dozens of fish staring back at him.

*They want those two jerks to stop*, Arthur thought. "They want you to stop!" Arthur didn't realize he had said that out loud.

Mike and Matt stopped and turned on their classmate.

"Really? You can talk to *fish* now?" Matt made his way to Arthur.

Mike shoved Arthur against the tank. "Freak. Why don't you tell the fish they're lame and only good for eating?"

*WHAM!*

Startled, the two bullies looked up at the glass dome above them. A ten-foot-long sand tiger shark stared down at the boys, teeth bared. The boys stopped in their tracks. The sand tiger shark charged again at the glass, this time causing it to form spiderweb cracks! The bullies ran to their teacher.

Arthur put his hand on the glass and took deep, controlled breaths. Almost instantly, the shark began to calm, its tail swishing slowly in the water. Hundreds of other sea creatures appeared then from the depths of the tank: stingrays, eels, sharks, squid, and a rainbow of fish. They all looked to him as if waiting for instructions. The shark closed its mouth, looked at Arthur, and seemingly gave a slight nod before swimming off.

"Lame? I'm sure he feels the same way about you two," Arthur said, a sly smile crossing his face as he walked past the two bullies, who were now white as ghosts.

Arthur's grin stayed on his face; he knew that the bullies would never bother him again.

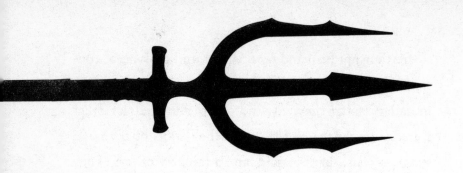

# ONE

*Stalnoivolk*, a six-hundred-foot Russian submarine, churned through the waters a few miles off the eastern Atlantic coastline, the seven blades of its propeller cutting through the sea like an underwater Ferris wheel. Attached to the side like a suckerfish was a sleek, high-tech miniature submarine, its white running lights flashing across its pitch-black hull. As sea life parted to get out of the massive sub's path, inside, the crew was seeking shelter from rapid machine-gun fire.

The emergency lights inside the control room cut out as the machine gun ceased fire and the alarms went silent. A middle-aged African-American man in a slick wet suit hoisted the gun to his shoulder, the barrel still smoking, as he stepped over the bodies of the dead Russian crewmen. Jesse Kane gave a wicked grin as he watched his band of pirates take their places at the ship's controls.

"Distress signal and all alarms have been disabled," came a voice from behind Jesse.

He turned to see a muscular, broad-shouldered younger version of himself, dressed in a heavily modified wet suit. The younger man's smile was even more dangerous than Jesse's, if possible. Jesse knew it was possible, because the man was his own son.

"Excellent, David. We're running dark again." Jesse nodded to the crewmen behind David, signaling them to bring their captive forward.

"But they heard it, of that you can be sure, American." The sub's captain was bloodied and beaten, yet still his voice was raised in defiance. This was a man who knew he was facing certain death, but who would fight to the bitter end, ready to go down with his ship. Jesse admired that in the man.

David sneered at the captain. "Make you a deal. I won't tell you how to captain, you don't tell me how to pirate."

He flicked his wrist and a long, lethal blade extended from the forearm of his suit. "On second thought, I'm not in the mood for deals today, so consider yourself relieved of duty."

As David wiped the blood from his blade, the captain's lifeless body fell to the floor, a gash cleanly cut through the front and back of his torso. Jesse was proud of the way his son took charge. He motioned for David to follow him as he walked to the officers' quarters at the bow of the ship.

David looked around at the empty bunks. "Where's the rest of the crew?"

"It seems our reputation precedes us. They've barricaded themselves near the torpedo bay ahead." Jesse reached into a pouch. "Or, I should say, *your* reputation. This was your op, your win. And I think you've earned this."

David looked at the item in his father's hand: a well-worn hunting knife. "I can't take that piece of junk. That's the love of your life. I've never seen you a day without it—sharpening that blade."

"It hasn't always been mine," Jesse said, placing the knife firmly into his son's hand. "It belonged to your grandfather. He was one of the navy's first frogmen in World War II and the first black man to have that honor. His fellow mates nicknamed him the Manta for how stealthily he moved through the water . . . and how quickly he could kill a man armed just with this knife." David turned the blade over and saw an image of a manta ray embossed into the handle. "He gave it to me when I was your age. I think he'd want you to have it now. Carry on the tradition."

David was about to thank his father when something thudded hard against the top of the sub, almost making them lose their footing.

Jesse activated the Bluetooth communicator in his earpiece. "What hit us?"

In the control room, one of the pirates was looking at the radar screen, his eyes not believing what they were seeing. "Sir . . . there's someone out there!"

"Another sub?" Jesse was confused. Even if help was coming, no vessel could have reached them this quickly.

"I think . . . it's a *man*!"

Before anyone could react, the behemoth submarine began to rise toward the surface! "I gave no order to change course!" Jesse barked.

With an amazing splash, the submarine broke the surface of the water and rose another ten feet into the air before crashing back down, floating like a lame, oversized metal duck. Inside, the pirates held their breath as they heard *footsteps* above them. Someone was walking on the hull!

A gleam in his eye, David turned to his father. "That's not a man."

"You think it's the 'Nessie' you've been chasing?" Jesse asked.

Before David could answer, there came the screeching sound of metal being ripped open. Jesse's men rushed to the sound. The top hatch was missing! They raised their guns tentatively, whispering among themselves. Without warning, the hatch flew down into the sub, knocking two pirates to the ground. A figure dropped from the hull into the sub.

Indeed, there was no man—no ordinary man at least. Towering above them with shoulder-length curly brown hair, golden eyes, and a bare broad chest covered in intricate tattoos, the mystery man stretched to his full height and gave a smirk.

"Permission to come aboard," said Arthur Curry.

The *rat-a-tat-tat* of gunfire from the pirates gave their answer. Arthur grabbed the hatch from the floor to use as a shield as he barreled down the sub's hallway. Bullets ricocheted as he continued his march like a football player headed for the end zone. He stopped in front of a cabin and tore the door off as though it were paper.

Turning to the last remaining pirate, he grinned. "Hold the door, will ya?" he asked as he threw it at the

pirate, flattening him. Arthur stepped into the room. It
was the torpedo bay where the surviving Russian crew had
hidden.

"He—he's real!" said one in Russian.

"And he's late for happy hour, so hurry up," Arthur
answered, also in Russian.

He led them up the stairs to the top of the submarine,
where they quickly boarded three lifeboats. "Stay here. Just
need to take out the trash." With that, Arthur dropped
back into the sub and found himself face-to-face with Jesse
and David, the elder pointing his machine gun and the
son with a Glock trained on the intruder's chest. The duo
opened fire.

As they emptied their weapons, round after round
knocking Arthur farther back, they drove him deeper
toward the torpedo bay. To escape the shower of bullets,
Arthur dropped through a hatch in the floor, deeper into
the bowels of the sub.

Arthur had only a moment to notice he was surrounded by the ship's torpedoes that lined the walls. He
caught a glimpse of an opening that had been cut with
laser-sharp precision. Beyond looked to be a control panel.
The mini submarine was docked there, attached securely so
as not to let in any water.

The *thunk* of another man dropping into the torpedo bay shifted Arthur's attention. It was the younger of his attackers. The man triggered a long blade that sprang from his suit's forearm. He gripped a short sword in his other hand, twirling it slightly. This attacker had a look of glee on his face as he started toward Arthur.

"Been waiting a long time for this," David said as he lunged.

Arthur dodged the blades deftly. "And yet this is the first time I've seen you. Couldn't have been waiting too long."

David engaged Arthur, crashing both blades down on him. Arthur blocked the move with a pipe he tore from the wall. The men's faces were inches apart. Arthur could see an odd excitement in the stranger's eyes.

"I scavenge the seas and you patrol them, right, 'Aquaman'? We were bound to meet sooner or later." David welcomed the challenge to face the creature he had studied for years, scouring reports and news about sightings of the mystery man from the sea. This indeed was his "Nessie," and he meant to make Arthur a prized trophy when he killed him.

"Huh. Well, let's not make a habit of it, then," Arthur said, pushing David back and dropping the pipe.

David slashed again and again at Arthur, who blocked the blades with his bare arms, knocking them aside without so much as a scratch. David's eyes widened as Arthur swung his forearm and knocked the short sword from David's grip. Dodging a swipe from the man's wrist blade, Arthur caught it between his hand and snapped it in two. David found himself hoisted in the air and Arthur flung him across the way. David's body slammed into the steel wall and slid down.

"You'll pay for that, fish man!" Arthur turned to face the voice in time to see Jesse standing behind him, grenade launcher in hand. With a *fwoom*, a grenade flew to Arthur's chest and exploded upon impact. The blast hurled Arthur against a wall, denting the metal where he hit, and he fell facedown.

Father and son exchanged glances, and smiles began to creep across their faces. The mighty hero of the sea had been downed. But the sound of metal scraping across the floor broke their silent celebration. Both men turned to see Arthur rise to his feet, pipe in hand.

Arthur brushed his long hair from his face, revealing a slight grimace. "Ouch." With an almost imperceptible flick of the wrist, the pipe flew from his hand and pierced Jesse's shoulder, pinning him to the opposite wall.

"Dad!" David stood in shock as Arthur walked toward Jesse.

"That's your kid? Talk about failing as a father." Arthur yanked the pipe out and Jesse slid down the wall, the gaping wound in his shoulder starting to bleed profusely. Arthur turned and began to climb the ladder back up to the main cabin.

"Don't talk to me about failure!" Jesse's scream echoed through the chamber as he tried to aim the grenade launcher at his ascending attacker. Injured, Jesse missed the mark wildly as the grenade sailed into the hull, blowing a hole in the ship and rattling a torpedo off the racks. The missile rolled mercilessly toward Jesse, crushing the man against the wall. The breach in the hull started to peel open, and water began to pour in.

David ran to his father and tried to lift the heavy metal that was pinning him. Looking to the ladder, he cried after Arthur, "You can't leave! He's trapped!"

Arthur barely looked down. "You boys got yourself in this mess, get yourselves out, 'scavengers of the seas.'"

"You can't just leave him like this!" David's voice howled as water began to rapidly rush in and fill the room. "He'll drown!"

This time, Arthur paused. His golden eyes flashed with

fury. "You murdered innocent people. Ask the sea for mercy."
With that, Arthur left them in the flooding chamber.

"Go," Jesse said. He sounded resolved to his fate, but
his son refused to stop trying to free him. Jesse lifted up a
grenade as David was about to protest. "You have to live so
you can kill him."

"I'll hunt him down and slit his throat like the Manta,"
David vowed.

Pulling the pin on the grenade, Jesse gave a weak smile.
"I expect nothing less, my son."

David cried out in anger as he felt his heart breaking.
"Damn you!" His voice echoed, and he hoped Arthur
could hear his curse.

David scrambled into the mini-sub, and looked back
one last time at his father. He hid tears as he closed the
hatch and detached from the giant craft. Looking behind
him, he saw a flash as the grenade exploded and the ship—
his father's watery casket—began to sink. David sped off,
thoughts of vengeance flooding his mind.

Arthur had already grabbed the lines of the three lifeboats
when he felt the ship rock from the blast in the torpedo
chamber. His face hardened. The sea had claimed the kill-
ers, as was its right.

Making sure the rescued Russian soldiers were secure in the rafts, he sped across the water, boats in tow, bringing the survivors to safety as the sun began its descent. *Mercy for the innocent*, he thought. The sea always had a way of ensuring balance, something Arthur had grown up hearing time and again from his father . . . among others.

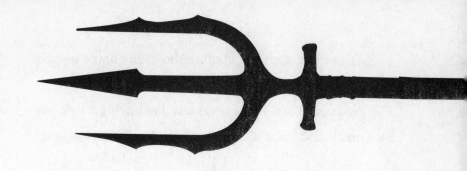

# TWO

The sun was rising on Amnesty Bay, and Tom Curry stood at the edge of the pier to greet it as he had for nearly thirty years. The wind blew through his short-cropped dark hair, now flecked with gray from the years, and the glow of the dawn lit his dark eyes. His tan skin was weathered with age. He smiled at the sea. *Tomorrow, maybe*, he thought. Tom turned and began walking back to the old lighthouse.

A loud splash broke the morning reverie. Tom's smile grew to a grin. Without turning back, he knew it wasn't Atlanna, but the tide had brought home the next best thing. "Welcome home, son."

"You're like a clock." Arthur shook his mane of hair dry as he joined his father.

"And you're in time for breakfast. I'm buying." Tom put his arm around his son, happy to have family home again.

Tom's well-worn red pickup truck was one of the few vehicles parked outside the tavern, the sign above the door reading "Terry's Sunken Galleon." It was the best place in Amnesty Bay to get greasy food any time of day or night without questions. Arthur and Tom were dining on such a feast as the televisions flashed cable news on the screens around the tavern.

Arthur looked at his father's plate, scraped clean, as he shoved a forkful of eggs into his mouth. "How is it I can breathe underwater but you can still swallow a whole meal before me?"

Tom shrugged, giving a crooked grin. "You've finally discovered my superpower."

The two men laughed. This felt . . . right. *It feels like home*, Arthur thought. He spent most of his time on the shores of other continents and had friends in many ports, but this, *this* was the only place he felt he could be himself.

"It's the top of the hour, and this morning's headline remains: 'Maritime Mystery!'" The news anchor's voice blared in the mostly empty bar. "Dramatic footage shows the navy aiding the rescued survivors of the *Stalnoivolk*, a Russian submarine apparently hijacked yesterday by a group of heavily armed and high-tech pirates that have been terrorizing the Atlantic lately."

The news caught Tom's attention, and he turned to watch the screen. Arthur glanced at the TV while chewing a piece of bacon. "These same pirates are wanted in connection with the disappearance of a prototype of a top secret naval mini–stealth submarine." An image of the sleek black ship flashed on the screen. It was the one Arthur had seen attached to the Russian ship.

"Wasn't me," Arthur murmured in response to his father's knowing look.

The anchor's voice chimed in as if on cue. "And we are getting unconfirmed reports that the 'meta-human' dubbed by social media as 'the Aquaman' was on the scene and likely the one responsible for this daring rescue." A blurry image of Arthur streaking across the sea, taken from a smartphone camera, filled the screen. Tom tilted his head slightly.

"Stand by that?" he asked, a smile beginning to form.

"That could be . . . anybody. The Bat?" Arthur countered unconvincingly.

"I don't think the Bat swims." Tom chuckled.

"No, he has some pretty crazy toys that do that for him," Arthur said under his breath.

Tom slapped his son's shoulder, leaving a greasy streak on his flannel shirt. He beamed. "You're doing it. You've *been* doing it, haven't you? What Vulko trained you to do?"

Arthur rolled his eyes at the name. "Vulko's only got one oar in the water."

Tom was undeterred. "I knew you'd embrace it someday. Your mother—"

"Stop. We've been over this."

"She always said you would be the one to unite the world with Atlantis," Tom finished. At the sound of the word, Arthur erupted.

*"Atlantis killed my mother!"* The harsh whisper carried a threat that the subject was still off-limits; old wounds ran deep.

Tom shook his head. "You don't know that."

"Has she returned? It's been almost thirty years! She's dead, killed because she gave birth to me, some half-breed no one wants in her former realm or here."

His father put his hand over Arthur's and forced him to face him. Softly, Tom said, "Son. One day you will have to stop blaming yourself for what happened."

Before Arthur could reply, a gang of five rowdy-looking bikers entered the Sunken Galleon. One turned to Terry behind the bar and barked for him to turn up the volume.

"It's that nut job I was tellin' you about. The underwater dude!" the biker told his friends.

The television now had two people on: the anchor and a man in a lab coat. "Joining us now to discuss his theories on this so-called savior of the seas is Dr. Stephen Shin, *formerly* of the US Institute of Marine Science. Thank you for joining us, Dr. Shin."

Dr. Shin looked as though he hadn't slept all night, anxious to have a platform to present his thoughts. "Thank you for having me."

"Dr. Shin," the anchor continued, "you have what some have called a rather *controversial* theory on this Aquaman's origin."

"Some may laugh it off, but may I remind you that three-quarters of Earth is covered by ocean. We spend billions to research life outside of this world, when, I ask, who's to say we are the only intelligent life on this land? Given what we've seen of him, we humans may not even be the most dominant species on Earth anymore." The scientist grew more and more animated as he spoke.

The blurry video still of Arthur filled the anchor's side of the screen again. "So you're suggesting Aquaman is from the *ocean*?" The anchor tried to suppress disbelief.

Dr. Shin leaned closer to the camera, eyes wide. "I am saying he is from *Atlantis*."

Arthur and Tom looked at each other nervously. Would anyone take this man seriously? The silent question was quickly answered as the bikers roared in laughter.

"See? What'd I say?" The leader of the gang wiped a tear from his eye as he nearly doubled over, cracking up at the idea.

The anchor's voice came over the speaker as Arthur's blurry photo remained. "To be clear, you're referring to the *myth* of—"

"The lost continent of Atlantis is no myth," Shin insisted. "Study tectonic plates; look at the landscape of Pangea. Once, we were all one supercontinent. Now there are seven, and Atlantis is the missing eighth! And populated by beings far more dangerous than anything from the stars. Just witness the video captured yesterday. This display of raw power is only the latest in . . ."

A chair scraped across the floor by the bar, accompanied by the group of bikers muttering among themselves. They were looking back and forth between the image on the screen . . . and Arthur.

"Yo!" the lead biker called, approaching the father and son, gang in tow. He put his hands on the table and leaned in. Nodding his head back to the TV, he asked, "That you? The fish boy?"

Arthur pushed his plate away and sighed. *Here we go*, he thought as he stood to face the man. He cocked an eyebrow.

"It's fish *man*." His look dared the men to push their luck further.

The lead biker reached into his vest and pulled out a cell phone. He cracked a wide grin. "Up for a selfie with me?" The biker laughed. The rest of the gang joined in.

"One with all of us! Hometown hero from under the sea," another roared.

Arthur wasn't sure if they believed the doctor or were just having a bit of fun. He looked at his dad. Tom shrugged. *Why not?* the two silently agreed.

"Terry!" Arthur motioned to the group. "Another round for these fools! On my tab." He turned back in time to see the flash go off as the lead biker leaned in for a photo.

The inhabitants of Terry's Sunken Galleon weren't the only ones tuning in to watch Dr. Shin try to explain the mysterious "Aquaman" and the possible connection to Atlantis. Floating off a deserted shore in the Atlantic was the stolen navy mini-sub. Inside, the walls and every surface were covered with pictures, news clippings, and printouts of articles. A giant map took up one wall, littered with pins in the places of Aquaman sightings, strings connecting each pin, tracking Aquaman's travels with twine. Dr. Shin wasn't the only one studying the man from the blurry video still that filled the onboard screens. However, *this* person knew Aquaman was real, from firsthand experience.

A printout of the blurry still was placed on the map, in the same spot where Aquaman had left David's father to die the day before. He stabbed it in place with his grandfather's manta knife. David seethed as the debate continued on the news.

"Listen to the man! Aquaman is alive, and he killed my dad! Why isn't anyone reporting *that*?" David's anger reached a boiling point.

Climbing out of the hatch to get some air, the pirate nearly fell back into the sub when he saw what was floating off the port side. A *man*, dressed in otherworldly armor, standing on the back of a ferocious shark! The man wore a helmet with water on the inside. When he turned

34

to address David, his voice boomed loudly through the helmet.

"It seems we have something in common. Rather, some*one*."

"What— Who are you? And how do you know me?" David silently cursed his broken blade and the knife stuck in the wall below him. He was unarmed and vulnerable to this tautly muscled creature.

"You can call me Murk." Murk stepped from the shark directly onto the surface of the water, and then onto the ship. David's jaw dropped. Murk looked down into the vessel, eyeing the pictures and map. "I think you already know where I come from."

"Doesn't answer how you know me," David said, recovering.

"We've been aware of you for some time. And"—Murk moved toward David—"I believe we may be of benefit to each other. Interested?"

"As long as it makes that damn Aquaman pay, I'm in." David's confidence grew as he realized he might have found a powerful ally.

Murk gave a smile that reminded David of a shark flashing its pointed teeth. "Revenge? Yes. But first we need something from you. A show of good faith, we'll call it."

As Murk extended his hand and David shook it, the man knew he had just entered into a pact that would change his life. One that would result in the end of Aquaman.

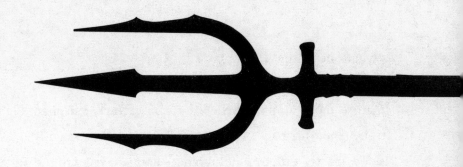

# THREE

**H**undreds of miles from where two men of different worlds met for the first time, another meeting was happening, deep in the depths of the sea. Breathtaking architecture lay in pieces, broken on the seafloor. Though a shattered, pale version of what it once was, these ruins were more remarkable than anything man had managed to build in the centuries since Old Atlantis had sunk. It was in these ruins that two contingents of different kingdoms had decided to come together for a momentous summit. That, at least, is what one of the leaders hoped.

Seated astride a massive *Tylosaurus*, a prehistoric creature most humans believed to be extinct, the man straightened his back. His chiseled jaw clenched slightly as his shortly cropped light blond hair swayed around the band that encircled his head. His ornate armor was polished to a shine, gleaming even underwater. Orm, king of Atlantis, gave his men one more look, ensuring everything and everyone was in the proper place. Atlantean guards, like those who had been sent to find Orm's mother decades earlier, rode great white sharks, each man armed with a hydro-pistol.

A man sidled up next to Orm's forty-five-foot-long steed, careful to avoid the flat tail lined with vicious barbs that whipped back and forth.

"Word, Vulko?" Orm addressed the man.

Vulko was older. He had served at Orm's father's side as royal adviser, a role he still maintained. Each line in his face was well earned and reminded him and those around him how seriously he took the safety and importance of the crown of Atlantis.

"He understands the significance of this meeting. Given the proposed terms, he will hear you out." Vulko crossed his arms, royal robes floating around him. His king looked at the procession advancing toward the clearing in the ruins.

King Nereus cut a commanding figure, well over six and a half feet, shoulders almost as broad as a fully grown tiger shark. His face was weathered from many battles, as his kingdom of Xebel existed in deeper, more treacherous waters than the glamorous New Atlantis. Each of Nereus's men rode astride an enormous seahorse, rider and steed armored in green. They parted for the great sea dragon that carried their ruler on its back in a mobile throne. King Nereus's chitinous-scaled armor seemed to absorb all light that came near him.

As his mount reached the center of the clearing, Nereus freed himself from his great carriage and swam to meet the approaching Orm and Vulko, both of whom had also dismounted. Nereus looked down at Orm for a tense moment before extending his arm. Orm clasped the man's thick forearm, and they shook in greeting.

"You've picked a meeting place too close to the surface for my liking, King Orm." Nereus cut to the chase.

Orm forced a smile. He had to play his hand carefully, which meant swallowing any perceived insults . . . for now. "You don't recognize the Council of the Kings?"

Surrounding them were seven massive statues, each

crumbling, in decay but still impressive. They were sculpted to represent seven different factions from across Atlantis.

"In Atlan's time, when the Seven Kingdoms were one, our ancestors gathered here. Atlantis stood here, royal Xebel by its side, as always. Together, all Seven Kingdoms ruled a state the world has yet to match."

Nereus gave Orm a curious look. "You speak as if our glory is behind us. Atlantis is still great." Nereus had to keep from spitting the last bit out. He, too, knew they were navigating intricate political waters.

"Atlantis is a mere shadow of what it once was. What it could *be*. Just as Xebel, too, can rise again." Orm began the pitch he had gone over for weeks. "I sit on a throne shackled by archaic rules and outdated policies. The Seven Kingdoms are too divided to see that a true threat is emerging. No longer can we believe, as our ancestors did, that hiding in our depths would protect us from surface dwellers. If we continue to cower in the shadows, deny our rightful place in the world, they will destroy us."

"Violence is a constant among surface dwellers. Given time, they will obliterate themselves," Nereus countered.

Orm nodded to Vulko, who produced a black, slickly

oiled mackerel from his robe. Pointing to the dead creature, Orm continued, "Their wars have already found
their way to our doorstep. Between their missile tests and
oil spills, they are daring to build machines that can dive
deeper than ever before. They seek constant conquest, as
you yourself said. If their pollution doesn't kill us, their
discovery of us will."

Vulko swam closer. "Atlantis is honored to invite the
great kingdom of Xebel to join in an alliance against the
surface." Vulko had decades of experience dealing with
negotiations, and it showed. He bowed his head slightly
before continuing, "And with the union of your daughter,
Mera, and our King Orm set, our bond will be closer than
ever."

Nereus thought on this. "Blood *is* thicker than water,
true." A look of concern crossed Nereus's face as he said
this, realization striking. "As sitting king of Atlantis, you
would claim the title Ocean Master under such an accord,
assuming you can secure alliances with two other kingdoms besides mine—"

"Only a title," Orm interrupted, wary of where this
was going.

"But what of the rumors that there is another Atlantean

who could lay claim to the throne? One of royal blood who walks among the surface dwellers. One who *defends* them?" Nereus could not keep the concern from his voice. He quickly discovered his words had struck a nerve with Orm. Vulko successfully covered his own shock that Arthur's existence had entered the equation. *I must plan for this accordingly*, he thought.

Face growing red, Orm did everything to hold his temper in check. Speaking through clenched teeth, he addressed Nereus. "My mother's bastard has never even been to Atlantis. His betrayal of us is even more reason to unite before he changes his mind and brings those he protects to us as his own army. This is why we must unite now, Ner—"

An explosion rocked the ruins as something collided with the outpost. The shock waves pushed both kings across the clearing. Vulko swam up to peer through the darkness and saw . . .

"Surface dwellers! Their submarine has discovered us! To arms," Vulko commanded.

Soldiers from both sides raced to their respective kings, encircling them in protection. A pillar fell as another torpedo impacted, closer this time. The heavy stone column scraped down Nereus's arm, nearly pinning it.

"Your king is injured," Orm cried.

The submarine fired a third torpedo. Orm, back on his mount, rode straight for it.

Nereus shook off his injury and grabbed a massive water cannon. He fired it at the oncoming missile. The cannon's blast collided against the metallic bomb. Orm zoomed past it, leaving the debris in his wake. He drew his royal trident from his armored back and hurled it at the massive craft's propeller. The blades shattered upon impact.

Hydro-pistols and Xebellian blasters cut and sliced the sub until it began to break into a dozen pieces, falling victim to the two kingdoms' finest soldiers. Had anyone taken the chance to go inside, they would have seen it was a ghost ship. Not a single body occupied the control room, which had Cyrillic writing on its walls. The six-hundred-foot Russian submarine sank for good this time.

Orm returned to the meeting place, his face glowing in rage. "There! We have not made war with them, but the surface dwellers just declared it upon us. Do you think otherwise now, King Nereus?"

The Xebellian king nodded in agreement. Wiping blood from his arm, he gave a somber vow. "They have sent their message. It is time we send the surface dwellers one in return."

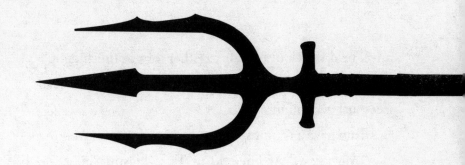

# FOUR

Terry's Sunken Galleon was the hottest spot as far as nightlife in Amnesty Bay. Not that it had much competition, considering it was pretty much the *only* spot for nightlife. *Tonight is no exception*, Arthur thought, as he exited the tavern, basically carrying his father more than helping him walk to the truck.

Tom looked at his son's intricate tattoos. "Hey," he said, a wild idea forming, "let's go home and work on your *moko*." Tom pointed to the triangular shapes that fit together in a tribal pattern. "If your pop-pop were still alive, he'd knock our heads together for not finishing it."

Arthur chuckled. "Plenty of time for that later, Dad. Let's just get you into bed."

Tom gave a thumbs-up and tried to focus on walking.

"You know," Arthur said to Tom, hoisting his father into the passenger side, "you're going to need to replace my old bed if I'm going to keep spending the night." He had to jiggle the troublesome seat belt until it finally clicked into place. It had been tricky for years, and now it was another thing to add to his growing to-do list.

"Yeah, I don't think that futon was built for *Aquaman*." Tom whispered the last word and gave a laugh.

Arthur shook his head. "Keep your voice down." He chuckled as he moved around the truck to the driver's seat.

"Yes," came a voice from the shadows. "You never know who might be listening."

Arthur started to raise his fist for a fight, then sighed, recognizing the measured tone in the stranger's voice. "Come on out, Vulko." The royal adviser emerged from the wooded area near the parking lot.

"I could never hide from you, could I, Arthur?" Vulko's eyebrow arched. "Especially when it came time for our talks about your place in the world."

"No. No, no, no. We are *not* having another discussion.

I know my place." Arthur could tell by the serious look on Vulko's face that there was a problem, and not one Arthur was interested in. "You trained me, I've been doing my thing up here, go me. You've been doing your thing down there, so go you. Seriously, go. You. Back there."

Vulko looked at Arthur, pride flashing across his face. "Indeed you have been doing your 'thing' up here, Aquaman. And quite well, from what I've heard." His face darkened. "But it is time for you to finally come protect your other home."

"*Home?!* Atlantis has never been my home! I've barely been to the outskirts, once, and I didn't even want to go except it was to save Earth. Up here, where my real home is." Arthur turned from Vulko and opened the truck door.

"Have you noticed the silence?" Vulko's words stopped Arthur in his tracks. "You can't sense them now, can you? The fish, whales, all the creatures who sing to you."

Arthur paused, cocking his head slightly. "They're . . ."

"Gone. Fled." Vulko's voice grew grave. "A surface craft attacked a meeting between two kings of the underwater kingdoms. They plan to retaliate. That reckoning is coming, Arthur."

"What's that got to do with me?"

"Because one of them is your brother."

Arthur's face hardened. "The only family I had in Atlantis died at the hands of her own kind. They murdered her, Vulko. They don't need me." Arthur defiantly got in the truck. "If you want to stop an attack, do it yourself."

As Arthur slammed the door shut, fired up the engine, and sped away, Vulko turned to the woods. "As I feared, words will not work on Atlanna's son. He's a fighter, like her."

"I'll take over," a softer yet determined voice spoke from the woods. "The waters are swelling. The fight is coming, and I'll be there to make sure he joins it."

Vulko trusted that if anyone could deliver on that promise, the figure could.

Arthur took the coastline road home, his father dozing in the passenger seat. As classic rock blared through the radio, he couldn't shake what Vulko had said. His old mentor was right: the sea was quiet. Deadly silent.

The radio began to crackle as the signal went dead. Arthur listened again and paled. The sea life might have grown silent or fled, but the water itself was suddenly roaring. As dozens of seagulls flew overhead, seeming to flee the ocean, Arthur's stomach dropped when he saw the view outside the passenger window.

The ships moored in the Amnesty Bay docks were rising, riding on a fifty-foot tidal wave! Arthur reacted quickly, scanning the road for higher ground. He knew Harbor Drive was a mile away. The hill it led to would provide enough safety to get the truck and his father away from the onrushing tide.

"Come on!" He gunned the engine, but the truck wasn't moving fast enough to outrun the wave. He braced himself for impact, protectively holding one arm across his father's chest.

Water engulfed the truck. Debris surrounded them. Arthur scanned for the quickest way out. The truck still had enough oxygen in it for his father to breathe as long as—

A tree trunk smashed through the windshield, slamming Arthur through the cab's back window! Stunned, Arthur tumbled in the undercurrent. Regaining his composure, he searched the churning tidal wave for the truck. There! Arthur swam, dodging trash cans, toppled telephone poles, and other obstacles the mighty water carried with it until he reached the truck. He tore the passenger door off and reached for his father—but Tom was gone! The seat belt was in tatters, and the driver's-side door was missing as well. Panicking, Arthur sped through the water to the other side. No sign of his father.

Before he could search more, he felt the sea move again. This time it felt as though it was tearing apart as it receded. He was in the middle of the parting tides, the sky suddenly visible, his feet finding purchase on solid ground beneath him. Looking around, he felt like what he imagined the followers of Moses must have seen as they walked through the parted Red Sea. The tidal wave rose ten feet in the air on either side of him and hung there, impossibly defying gravity. With a lurch, the waves began to move back in the direction of the sea.

As the water made its march back to where it belonged, Arthur looked ahead. Backlit by a lamppost, a figure stood, arms raised. From a distance, Arthur could see that her eyes and hands were glowing a shocking shade of electric blue. At her feet, before him, lay his father. Arthur rushed to Tom and the woman, his attention turning back to his father.

Kneeling, he put his head to Tom's chest. "Damn it! He isn't breathing!"

"Let me." The woman's voice was calm.

Not taking his eyes off his father, he saw the woman place her hand gently on Tom's chest. Tom's mouth opened and water, spiraling like a funnel, shot out. Tom began to cough. Arthur quickly lifted Tom's neck to allow as much air as possible to enter the man's lungs. Tom gasped, his eyes fluttering open.

"Thank you," he said weakly. Arthur was about to reply when he realized his father wasn't looking at him, but at the woman behind him.

Arthur turned and finally took in the woman. Fiery red hair lit the air around her. The moonlight accentuated her pale skin, flesh so milky white it looked as though it had never been touched by sunlight. She was dressed in a skintight green wet suit. Armor, Arthur corrected himself. Looking into her deep green eyes, his eyes widened in recognition. He had encountered her once before, during a great undersea battle he'd rather have forgotten, on the outskirts of Atlantis.

"You," he breathed.

"We meet again, Arthur Curry, son of Atlantis," the woman said.

Arthur shook his head. "Thanks for saving my dad, but *he* is the only father I belong to."

The woman gestured to the devastation surrounding them. "You honestly can't think this was natural."

"I'm sure it wasn't, but you and me, we're even now. I saved you; you saved my dad. We're done." Arthur turned to tend to his father.

"Your half brother, Orm, king of Atlantis, wants war with the surface world!"

"Nothing I can do about that except stay here and protect my friends and family." Arthur was firm.

The woman crossed her arms. "The son of Atlanna turns his back on his people and chooses to bury his head in the sand like an oyster?"

"They are *not* my people! Vulko already tried this speech and I turned him down. You're not getting a different answer from me, lady. Go back to Atlantis and be with your own kind."

"I am not Atlantean. I am Princess Y'Mera Xebella Challa." She stood proudly.

Arthur gave her a curious look. "Xebellian? Even more reason for you to go back. Get your kind to stop Orm, *Princess*."

"Mera's fine. And I can't. My relationship with Orm and Atlantis is . . . complicated."

Arthur scoffed. "And I'm supposed to uncomplicate it?"

"You're supposed to take your rightful place on the

throne as the firstborn son of Queen Atlanna."

Arthur raged. "How many times do I have to say this? Atlantis killed my mother. What makes you think they'd accept her bastard on the throne? I'm no king."

"I agree," Mera said flatly. "But you *could* be. Vulko thinks so, at least."

Arthur shook his head. "Vulko has delusions of grandeur when it comes to me. Always has."

Tom placed his hand on his son's face and turned it toward him. "Arthur. You have the pride of your mother. I've always said that. Now tap into her compassion and honor." His voice grew stronger. "She returned because it was her duty."

"My duty is to stay here and protect you," Arthur protested.

"Protect me, protect *all* of us, by making sure something like tonight's tragedy never happens again."

Mera's voice echoed Tom's sentiments. "This was Orm's doing. It will only get worse as his war against the surface grows."

Arthur stood to face her. "You saved my father and probably a lot more people tonight. Thank you."

"You'll come with me?" Mera was hopeful.

Arthur's face hardened. "Not for you," he said, his voice turning grave. "I'm going with you to stop my brother before he hurts anyone else."

Arthur helped his father to his feet, Mera following them. Arthur's mind was filled with dark thoughts, knowing he would be dragged to a land he never wanted to see, to face a brother he never wanted to meet.

Hundreds of miles off the coastline, floating in international waters, David Kane was once again lying atop his stealth mini-sub as it floated on the water. He wondered, as he had for over a week now, when the Atlanteans would fulfill their end of the bargain. He listened as the talking heads on the news debated about the nature of the catastrophic—and baffling—series of tidal waves that had flooded coastal cities.

". . . unprecedented reports from all over the world continue to pour in," said one.

"The US, Great Britain, Canada, China. Images of warships and civilian crafts washed ashore. Mounds of waste and barrels dumped into the ocean now forced back on land as if the sea suddenly has a mind of its own," blared another.

". . . no way this could have been natural. Not only is

it unprecedented, but it goes against the very laws of physics. Could this have been coordinated? If so, by who . . . or what?" The news anchor who had reported the Russian submarine rescue had Dr. Shin on his show once again.

The doctor was speaking calmly now. The global tides seeming to attack as one gave him a renewed sense of affirmation and validity. "You're correct. These were not natural. Every city attacked had warships docked. All are world powers. This clearly was an attack."

"Are you proposing your Atlantis theory again, Doctor?" The reporter seemed slightly less skeptical this time.

"I'm sure you can agree, sir, this is no longer a theory. Tonight, Atlantis made itself known, and its agenda is clear. This was a declaration of war!" Dr. Shin sat back to let his words sink in for the viewers around the world watching.

David gave a rare smile. The world was in chaos, and it refused to believe what he knew was a fact: Dr. Shin was one hundred percent right. And David was at the center of it all.

His moment of revelry was broken by the sight of the sea suddenly lit beneath him. Looking overboard, he saw an enormous foreign craft just below his sub. It was magnificent: technology light-years beyond anything the surface had accomplished. *At last*, he thought, *reward*.

He turned in time to see Murk walking across the water and onto David's ship. He carried a large sack, David noted. "It worked?"

"That should be obvious to you. But you have a different question in mind. One that can be answered by my king." Murk took out a device and tossed it onto the water's surface. Immediately, the water rose up and arranged itself to form a figure, regal and strong.

Orm, a water hologram of him at least, addressed David. "Your assistance is appreciated. The submarine attack did what was needed. I thought it would have been intact, though. My men nearly noticed the gaping hole in its side."

"You're lucky I was able to even salvage that, much less get the remote systems online to pilot it from here," David said, irritated. "And that 'gaping hole' is where your *Aquaman* left my father to die!"

Orm's face contorted briefly before regaining its composure. His annoyance was clear, even through the water-churned vocal projector. "He has nothing to do with this. Murk, give the man his payment. Our business is concluded."

"Wait!" David yelled as the water hologram dissolved

into mist before his eyes. "What about my revenge?"

Orm's disembodied voice came from the disc floating on the sea. "This should cover enough for you to wage your personal war. I have more global matters to attend." With that, the lights switched off. David's audience with the king of Atlantis was over.

Murk dropped the sack on the hull of the ship. The moonlight caught the glint of hundreds of gold coins inside.

"You promised me Aquaman." David scowled at Murk.

"I said you would have your chance." He pointed to the gold. "Here is your means to that."

"I want that fish-face's head!" David yelled at Murk's back as the Atlantean walked from the sub. As Murk began to sink into the sea to his own vessel, a grin spread across his face. Orm believed he could take care of Aquaman should the need arise, but Murk knew they had just bought something better: a pawn.

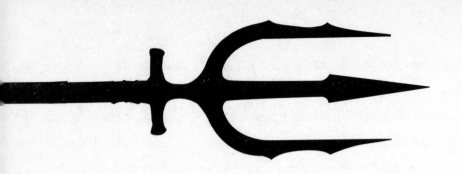

# FIVE

The unlikely trio had made their way back to the lighthouse—a woman who lived beneath the sea, a surface dweller, and his son, who straddled both worlds. Arthur was tending to Tom's injuries—minor scrapes and bruises, remarkably—when he heard Mera's voice coming from the living room.

"Yes, the safe house near Gateway Bridge. He is joining us, Vulko . . . for vengeance now, but once he is there . . . Yes, that's my hope as well. We'll see you soon." Mera clicked off her communicator just as Arthur leaned against the doorway, clearing his throat.

"Vulko, huh? I should've figured you two were tag-teaming me." Arthur didn't seem surprised.

Mera looked at him, exasperated. "We only want what is best for Atlantis, and for you."

"Fine," she continued. "If not for Atlantis, then for your precious surface world. This is the only way to—"

"'End a war, save the world, blah blah.' Heard it from Vulko, and gods know you've drilled it into my head." Arthur rolled his eyes.

The two stared at each other, as if daring the other to push further. Mera broke her gaze and began to walk out. Arthur followed.

The full moon shone bright on the pair as they stood on the pier. The storm had passed, after causing so much destruction. Arthur turned his gaze to the rocky cliffs nearby, his gaze going farther, deeper, than just a passing glance.

"That is where my father found my mother. It was storming, like earlier." His voice was soft. It changed quickly, though, growing bitter. "It's also where Atlantis came to retrieve her."

"I-I've heard the stories of her time here. Of your birth." Mera tried to connect with him, but this seemed only to turn his anger toward her.

"I'm a legend, then? My mother said I would be . . . before Atlantis demanded their queen. Before they killed her," Arthur said through gritted teeth.

Mera knew not to push him on the matter. He was coming to Atlantis, which was her mission. She heard a strange sound come from him: a chuckle.

"What?" she asked.

"It's also the place where another Atlantean came to me and asked me to take a dive." Arthur smiled. "Gods, I was young. And stupid."

His voice trailed off at the memory, lost in thoughts of years long past.

A thirteen-year-old Arthur Curry climbed the rocks of his home shore and made his way to the top of a cliff. He walked to the man standing at the edge, waiting for him. The man's tunic and pants were impeccably tailored and shimmered in the noon light, as though made of delicate fish scales. Arthur looked down from the cliff, the sea's tide going in and out, crashing upon rocks. The ocean stretched out, vast and powerful, all the way to the horizon, where water met sky.

"Are you sure about this, Vulko?" Arthur asked, his hair whipping in the wind.

His voice as calm as the low tide, Vulko turned to his pupil. "You must forget all the teachings of the surface world. Do not think about oxygen—you already know you can breathe underwater. Do not worry about pressures from the depths; they can't hurt you—your true Atlantean nature lies deep near the bottom of the sea."

"But I already know how to swim." Arthur eyed the drop-off with caution.

Vulko smiled. "Not even close."

Raising his arms, Vulko looked at Arthur. "Do as I do. Ready . . . and *jump*!"

Arthur raised his arms and followed his mentor's instructions. His legs, more powerful than any average teen's, vaulted him up and over the cliff. He saw Vulko enter the water without a splash. Arthur tucked his head instinctively, and his body formed a perfect line, allowing him to slice through the ocean surface without disturbing it and propel deeper than he'd gone before. He had reached the depth where he would normally turn back, the place where the light dimmed in the sea, when a hand stopped him.

"Being Atlantean means more than just being able to breathe underwater," Vulko said. Arthur was constantly amazed that he could hear him and speak without breathing. "Your body is equipped to withstand freezing depths."

The pair dived deeper, until the sun barely penetrated the waters.

"Let your eyes adjust to your surroundings. You don't need light to see an entirely different world exists here." Arthur followed Vulko's instructions and felt his sight shift. His eyes turned a golden hue, and his vision cleared, revealing an entirely new world. Suddenly, the ocean came alive! Bright, bold colors of coral. Exotic fish that never came near the surface swam in schools. Algae lit the rocks they clung to. Arthur could feel a rhythm to the way everything seemed to sway and ebb and flow. There was order, there was harmony, and there was even danger. This was truly a different world, and he was a part of it.

"This is awesome!" Arthur beamed.

"Oh, would you like to see awesome?" Vulko grinned, turned away from his rapt student, and—*BOOOOM!*—he was tearing through the water, leaving a circular wake behind him.

*Challenge accepted*, thought Arthur, as he let his body take over. With a similar *boom*, he jetted off in Vulko's direction, his feet moving impossibly fast, propelling him after his teacher.

Together they swam up and over great white sharks, around a herd of hammerhead sharks, alongside a group of turtles migrating, until Vulko turned down, going deeper. Without warning, he shot back up, body ramrod straight, headed for the surface. Arthur mimicked the older man's actions and felt the surface of the water crack as he broke through, soaring fifty feet into the air.

Oxygen filling his lungs, Arthur let out a "WHOOO-HOOO!" like only a thirteen-year-old could. He looked down and saw a funnel of water trailing behind him, droplets falling on the rocks below.

Day turned to night, and Arthur had spent the whole time exploring the sea and honing his newfound skills. He could feel the animal life and he sensed they welcomed him as part of their world below the surface. He came face-to-nose with a dolphin and gently reached out. The dolphin nuzzled him and swam closer. From his spot on the beach, Vulko saw Arthur break the surface, astride the dolphin's back. Arthur steered it to the pier he knew so well. Home.

Vulko was sitting at the edge, smiling with pride.

"Vulko," Arthur began, "when can I meet my mother?"

Vulko's smile strained. "Soon, my young prince. When you're ready, I'll take you to Atlantis to meet the queen."

Arthur let out yet another whoop—Vulko had lost

count of how many times he'd heard the boy yelp in excitement that day—and rode the dolphin farther out.

"Just so we're clear," Arthur said, turning his attention back to the present, "I'll help you stop this war, but then I'm done. Out."

Mera faced him, her annoyance clearly showing. "Perhaps that's for the best," she spat back.

"A war, huh? I think you'll need this, then." Tom's calm voice broke the tension as the two turned to look at the man walking down the pier. He was holding a familiar object in his hand.

"Mother's trident." Arthur cocked an eyebrow at his father.

"She'd rather you use it than it be a fancy wall decoration." Tom smiled.

Mera tried to hide her awe at the sight. "Queen Atlanna's trident. She was one of Atlantis's fiercest warriors, especially with that in her hand."

"She was. And will be again." Tom's unwavering faith in her return deflected any questioning glances either of the other two threw his way.

"You sure you're okay, Dad? That was a crazy undertow," Arthur asked, taking the trident from his father.

Tom smiled and playfully swatted his son's hand away from the bandage on his head. "I've lived through worse. Believe me." He turned to Mera.

"This young man is destined to be more than just a tool for stopping a war. You make sure he fulfills what destiny awaits him." Tom's voice had turned serious.

Mera placed a closed fist over her heart and gave a brief nod, a silent vow. The gesture did not go unnoticed by Arthur.

"I'm going down for one thing, and then it's back to here. There's no Terry's in Atlantis." Arthur smiled and pulled his father in tight. "Can't leave my best friend alone up here."

Tom tousled his son's long brown hair and smiled. "I love you, too. Now go make your mother and me proud."

Arthur turned away, and though he would deny it, a slight tear welled up briefly.

"Where's your ship?" he muttered to Mera.

"Dive down. I'll lead," she answered. As Arthur dived into the water, Mera looked back to see Tom. The man had two reasons to rise and greet the dawn on this pier now. She silently prayed that she could bring one of them back safely.

Arthur Curry was immovable. He looked at the Xebellian submersible—a craft that looked like it had an exoskeleton and razor-sharp fins—but it wasn't an objection to the ship itself that kept him from entering it. Rather, it was where Mera had chosen to hide it that had Arthur digging his heels in. The sunken cargo container was a clever idea; Arthur had to give her credit there. However, it had tipped over in the tidal wave attacks and was now coated with dead fish.

"Holy mackerel!" Arthur's exclamation came from both surprise at the craft's sleek and unique design as well as at seeing the layer of dead fish.

"Fish puns? Now? Really?" Mera scowled as she reached into her craft and turned it on. As the lights began to glow, a slight hum started. The fish were blown off at once.

Arthur smiled, knowing he was getting under her skin. It was the least he could do, considering she was taking him to the one place he'd sworn he would never go.

He entered the craft on the passenger side. Mera's ship shot out of the container before Arthur was even settled.

Traveling at a speed faster than Arthur had ever swum, Mera's sub rocketed through the depths of the water.

"This is probably the farthest down you've ever been." It was not a question.

"Not quite," Arthur said. A moment later, he saw a sea creature he had never laid eyes upon before.

"Okay, I take it back. *This* is the farthest I've been."

Mera revved the engine faster and did not bother trying to hide her smile. "It only gets deeper before we reach Atlantis."

Arthur managed not to throw up his dinner. "Wonderful."

Fortunately, he didn't have to hold it down much longer. The ship slowed suddenly and smoothly. Arthur, who had vowed for years that he would never set foot here, who had cursed its existence and sworn himself an enemy of the place, now took in his first glimpse of Atlantis. He couldn't contain the slight gasp as his breath caught.

"Welcome home," Mera said, without looking at him, a smile tugging at her lips. "Arthur, prince and rightful heir to the throne of Atlantis."

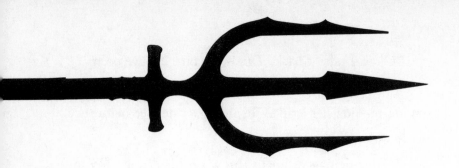

# SIX

As a child, Arthur dreamt of Atlantis, imagining a place of wonder and, most important, his mother. As an adult, Atlantis plagued his nightmares, a twisted and corrupted undersea nation responsible for killing his mother. As he looked upon it at last, Arthur realized he had never known Atlantis. No one could.

Atlantis was beyond anything in the realm of imagination.

Stretching for miles, built upon giant rock and coral formations, nestled in a vast canyon, interconnected by active pathways, were buildings that looked as though they had been pulled from the ocean floor and crafted into shining, multilevel dwellings. Illuminating the city with a bioluminescent glow were tens of thousands of jellyfish, ranging in size from a foot in diameter to one hundred feet across, floating in place. Surrounding the capital city was a massive wall; the only entrance flanked by two impossibly large statues, each a proud warrior.

Rising a mile high in the center of this magnificent city was a pointed spire that appeared to be made of pure silver. It was lit by radiant energy that pulsed from it and through the city. At the base was a large opening with a circular energy wheel lighting what appeared to be a grand throne room, open on three-quarters so that whoever sat on the throne could gaze out upon the massive kingdom.

Arthur turned to Mera, his jaw so open she thought his beard might touch his lap. She simply smirked in response.

Mera brought the ship closer to the wall. Looking around, Arthur saw all manner of races he'd never encountered before, riding various sea creatures or in vehicles that those on the surface could never have dreamt up. There were mer-creatures that were half humanoid, half fish or shark or dolphin—any number of combinations, Arthur noted—some humanoid on the top half and even some reversed in their combinations. All were headed to the gates of Atlantis's capital city.

Arthur reflexively gripped his mother's trident harder as his eyes fell upon figures from his darkest childhood nightmares. Although he was only three years old when he saw them last, the image of Atlantean guards in their white-and-silver armored suits was seared in his brain. Surrounding the wall were dozens of these sentries, mounted on large armored sharks.

"Why build a wall and bridge underwater?" Arthur asked, tearing his gaze from the soldiers.

"The Gateway Bridge is a remnant of the old world. And it's the only way in or out of Atlantis." Mera was still surprised at how little the son of Atlantis's former queen actually knew of his birthright kingdom.

Arthur snorted in derision. "Can't they just *swim* over the wall?"

"Security getting into the city is impenetrable. Even if someone were to sneak past the guards, they'd never make it far enough to evade the hydro-cannons." Arthur gave her another questioning glance at this.

"People are always trying to get into Atlantis. Everyone wants to live in the greatest capital in the world." Mera's voice was filled with wonder at the last part. Arthur let out another grunt, not swayed by her words.

They approached a border guard at his check post. Tension rose in Arthur again. Sensing this, Mera waved a hand. "Don't worry, I have diplomatic clearance."

Arthur was sardonic. "Right. Princess. Almost forgot."

Mera ignored him as they moved into Atlantis proper. Neither noticed the border guard as he gave her ship a second glance, raised his scanning device, and recorded their entrance. He punched in a code, and the scan was beamed to his superiors, Mera and Arthur none the wiser.

The city was even more astounding inside. Arthur turned to see crustaceans as tall as him walking about. Even more sea-animal/humanoid varietals jostled and navigated their way through the city, swimming in lanes that went in all directions, at all angles. His head whipped around as he caught sight of a hydro-powered train zooming past, filled with more residents.

Once they were sufficiently away from the wall and mixed in with the crowds, Mera spotted a clear path and angled her craft down into the deeper parts of the city. Here the city grew darker as the bioluminescence of the jellyfish and other creatures above faded. The craft's lights revealed a far different world than what existed mere meters above. Crumbling ruins littered broken paths that looked as though they were once streets. Arches cracked, rubble blocking whatever entrances remained to the buildings that once stood there. There were carvings similar to the warrior statues that stood towering above, but these were more simplified, and long forgotten.

"Guess the cleaning crew forgot this area," Arthur said.

"This is what's left of the Old City," Mera offered by way of explanation. "There's a safe house here. The Highborns never venture to the seafloor."

"Highborns?" Arthur raised his eyebrow. "Seriously?"

Mera ignored him, pointing to a hulking shadow ahead. "We're here."

As they grew closer, Arthur realized they were steering into a blown-out hole in the side of a huge sunken sailing vessel, centuries old. Like the residents surrounding it, the ship was long forgotten. Docking alongside it, Mera and Arthur—still holding his trident—ejected from her ship and swam into the blown-out hole. As they entered, Arthur felt the water . . . end. Suddenly, he was standing on the floor of the ship, breathing oxygen again.

"PUT TWO SHIPS IN THE OPEN SEA, WITHOUT WIND OR TIDE,

AND, AT LAST, THEY WILL COME TOGETHER."

—JULES VERNE

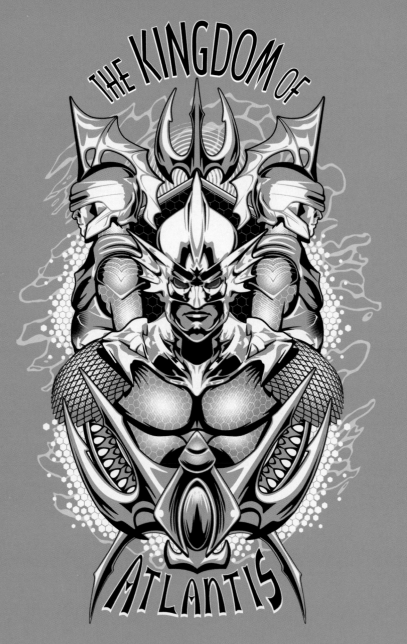

THE KINGDOM OF

ATLANTIS

"A WAR IS COMING TO THE SURFACE WHETHER YOU LIKE IT OR NOT, AND I'M BRINGING THE WRATH OF THE SEVEN SEAS WITH ME."

—ORM, KING OF ATLANTIS

THE KINGDOM of
XΣBΣL

LONG AGO, WHEN THE SEVEN KINGDOMS WERE
ONE, ATLANTIS STOOD WITH ROYAL XEBEL
BY ITS SIDE, AS ALWAYS.

# THE BRINE KINGDOM

TOGETHER, ALL SEVEN KINGDOMS
RULED A STATE THE WORLD HAS
YET TO MATCH.

# THE TRENCH KINGDOM

"HE SACRIFICED HER TO THE CREATURES
OF THE TRENCH, THOSE THAT DWELL WHERE
LIGHT CANNOT PENETRATE THE DARKNESS,
AND FROM WHICH NO ATLANTEAN
HAS EVER RETURNED."

—MERA, PRINCESS OF XEBEL

# BLACKMANTA

"DID YOU THINK YOU COULD LEAVE
ME THERE TO DIE AND FORGET ME?"

—BLACK MANTA

"THE ORIGINAL TRIDENT COULD ONLY BE
WIELDED BY THE STRONGEST ATLANTEAN.
IT GAVE KING ATLAN MASTERY OVER
THE SEVEN SEAS."

—ATLANNA, QUEEN OF ATLANTIS

# UNITE THE KINGDOMS

ONE DAY, A NEW KING WILL RISE TO POWER.
WITH THE LOST TRIDENT OF ATLAN, HE WILL
RESTORE THE SEVEN KINGDOMS INTO
A UNIFIED ATLANTIS.

"What—?" Arthur looked around. Everything around them was dry!

"An added layer of protection," Mera said, pointing to the bubble that Arthur now noticed surrounded the ship. "Only Highborns can breathe in both water and air, thus the pocket barrier."

"Plus," a voice came from the shadows, "it helps keep the animals out." Vulko stepped into the light, revealing himself. He was beaming at the sight of Arthur.

Arthur gave his mentor a smirk. "Finally got your wish, Vulko. I'm here."

Darkness crossed Vulko's face. "I only wish it were under better circumstances."

"I can't believe Orm attacked—" Mera blurted out as Vulko raised a hand to stop her.

"Oh, that wasn't an attack. It was a warning to the surface world."

"Provoked by what?" Mera asked.

"Your father and King Orm were attacked by a surface submarine. It fired upon them as they met in the old King's Gathering."

"What?!" Arthur was incredulous. "That's impossible. To the surface, Atlantis is just a myth. An old wives' tale at best.

They'd have no way of knowing how or where to attack!"

Vulko gave Arthur a sad look. "I was there."

Arthur and Mera were stunned by this. A first-hand account?

"Nereus now sides with Orm." Vulko delivered the news to Mera, who looked down, shoulders slumped for the first time since Arthur had met her. Vulko turned to Arthur. "If we're to prevent this war, you must dethrone Orm now."

Arthur looked at Vulko as if he'd grown fins. "You want me to become *king*?! I was just supposed to come down here and beat some sense into a half brother I've never met. Or clear the way for *you*, Vulko."

"The throne is not mine to claim, but it is yours. By birthright."

Vulko had given him the same argument multiple times as he had tried to convince Arthur to join him in Atlantis.

Arthur scoffed. "They don't know me. How could they ever accept a half-breed as their king? If I even wanted it."

"By winning over the people. Orm rules by might. You are driven by your mother's side: heart." Vulko placed a piece of aged sharkskin on a nearby table. It had been used as paper, an ornate trident drawn on the surface. "And by retrieving this."

Arthur lifted his own trident. "Already got one, thanks."

Vulko smiled, a gleam in his eye. "Not like this one. This is the *Lost Trident of Atlan*." Vulko spoke with a reverence Arthur had never heard.

Arthur gave him a pointed look. "I know this one. It's the only story my mother told me that I remember. I used to pretend I was Atlan, waving around a wooden fork, like a complete dork." Arthur's face flushed in embarrassment as he let that last part slip.

"You brought me down here to chase after a bedtime story?" he asked, annoyed now.

"The surface world thinks Atlantis is a bedtime story, do they not?" Mera asked, a sly grin crossing her face. Checkmate. "That *is* what you said, right?"

"That's different," Arthur snapped back.

"Is it?" Vulko asked, playing referee. "This is just as real as the impossible city above you."

"All right. So Atlan's mighty trident was the most powerful thing down here, if I'm remembering. Then he got all power-mad and Atlantis broke apart and sank into the Seven Kingdoms." Arthur stifled a grin as he caught Mera's impressed look. "Now, I'll bite. What happened to it?"

"It disappeared with Atlan. Disgraced, he left Atlantis to live his days in exile, taking the trident with him, fearful that another might abuse its power," Vulko said.

"But if we can retrieve it, the bearer of Atlan's trident can unite the Seven Kingdoms once again," Mera said, optimism creeping into her voice.

Arthur remained unconvinced. "If it's so powerful, why hasn't Orm gone after it?"

"Because he would rather rule the Seven Kingdoms by sheer force, uniting them under a banner of fear and war." Vulko's voice was grave. "A goal he is close to achieving. And a war that only you can stop, for only a descendent of Atlan may wield the trident—a son of Atlanna."

"Atlantis *killed* my mother for giving birth to me! No ancient fork is going to change that, even if I could find it!" Arthur erupted.

Vulko pulled out a cylinder from the folds of his robe. "Loyalists of your mother—yes, they exist—have been scouring the seas for clues. They recently found this. It's an ancient codex that needs further translation. It bears a destination on it. Not the location of the Lost Trident, I fear, but we believe it leads to a clue to where the trident can be found."

As Vulko was about to hand the canister to Arthur, the trio heard a loud *BOOM* from the other side of the ship, followed by voices.

"Last scans indicate they came this way. Must be here somewhere." The voice was muffled, as if spoken through a helmet. As the meaning of that dawned on Arthur, panic crossed Vulko's face.

"Atlantean guards!" he hissed.

"How? I thought you said so-called Highborns don't come down here." Arthur was confused, though he raised his trident, preparing for battle.

Vulko winced. "I may have been followed," he whispered. "Since the surface attack, Orm has been paranoid—security has been airtight." He jammed the paper into Mera's hand then grabbed her arm. "Hurry, Princess. You mustn't be discovered down here."

"What about *me*?!" Arthur hissed back as the two ran around a corner. He was about to follow them when a concussive blast of water blew him back, slamming him against the wall. Blearily, he looked at his approaching attackers, their cannons aimed at him.

A smile crossed the face of one, dressed differently from the rest. His armor was more ornate and skintight. His slender yet muscular body seemed to glide as he walked to Arthur and knelt down, face-to-face with his prisoner.

"Welcome home, Aquaman. Yes, I'm quite aware of who you are. I am Murk, captain of the Royal Guard. In the name of His Highness, King Orm, I place you under arrest." Murk's almond-shaped eyes were alight with joy at his capture. With a flash, they changed to a violent glare as he jammed a shock baton into Arthur's chest, sending a painful jolt of electricity through his body.

Arthur stiffened in shock and two guards approached the stunned hero. Murk grabbed Arthur by the hair, expecting to find an unconscious land dweller.

Arthur was smiling.

"That was supposed to hurt? Cute." Swiftly, Arthur hit Murk in the jaw with a massive uppercut. He grabbed the stun baton and ran up the wall behind him, flipping at the last second, parkour-style, to land behind them. With a one-two jab to each, he felled the Atlantean guards.

Arthur was turning to tell Mera and Vulko it was safe when he saw a blur of motion. A series of kicks bashed him repeatedly in the face: Murk's training as captain of the Royal Guard was in full display. Arthur slumped back to the ground.

"Cute moves yourself. But I'm better." Murk upped the voltage in the stun baton and slammed it again in Arthur's chest. This time, Arthur fell to the ground.

The last thing Arthur saw as he drifted into unconsciousness was Mera's ship, through a small port window, speeding into the distance.

Waking, Arthur found himself in chains, shackled to a dungeon wall. It was filled with water, cavernous and rocky. He looked around and saw other prisoners lining the walls as far as he could see. None of them were human— non-Highborns, Arthur guessed.

He turned to the prisoner on his left, a decrepit wreck of a creature, a humanoid puffer fish, whose spines looked as though they had been ripped out violently.

"Don't suppose you're down here for planning a regime change, too, huh?" Arthur asked the creature. It turned away from him, terrified to even look Arthur in the eye. "Worth a shot. S'okay, I got a few friends here . . . somewhere."

The sound of armored guards approaching alerted Arthur that he was not receiving friendly visitors. The guards kicked the puffer fish creature, even though it wasn't in the way.

Arthur yanked at his chains, enraged. "What the hell was that for? Look at him! He couldn't hurt anyone, unlike me. I'm going to—" The shock from a baton coursed through Arthur's body, halting what it was he planned to do—something likely involving ripping limbs from the guards' bodies.

Stunned, Arthur could barely lift his head as the guards unshackled his chains from the wall and began to swim upward, out of the dungeon, dragging Arthur behind them. The light ahead grew blinding to Arthur as they swam up a corridor and through an ornate door.

Suddenly, Arthur found himself flung to the ground. Four guards surrounding him chained each arm and leg to the floor, forcing Arthur to kneel before their king. The glow of a giant energy wheel made it difficult for Arthur to focus. Gathering his bearings, he struggled against his chains, but the guards kicked him back. Arthur looked around, noting he was on a dais made of gleaming polished silver. His stomach sank as he remembered seeing this place from a distance when he first entered Atlantis in Mera's ship.

He knelt at the foot of a dozen steps, atop which was a throne on a large platform. On that throne sat a man with chiseled features and shortly cropped flaxen hair. The man was looking down at him, a menacing grin crossing his face. The man spoke, and Arthur's blood rose at the words.

"Welcome to Atlantis, Brother."

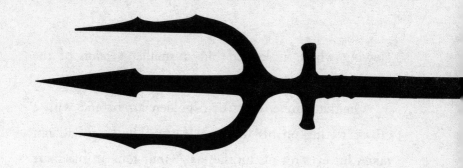

# SEVEN

The throne room stretched out to nearly fifty feet, side to side, by Arthur's estimation. The platform on which the throne sat was at least twenty-five feet across, with seating on either side of the throne. The throne itself had seven spikes rising above it in the shape of a trident, each spike representing one of the Seven Kingdoms, with the middle spire, presumably Atlantis, rising higher than the others. Arthur thought the throne looked spotless, as if meticulously polished. Two wings stretched out beyond the dais in either direction. Behind the throne was a giant glowing wheel. It looked like a smaller version of the battery that powered the capital city.

On the throne, dressed in golden armor and with a crown resting on his head, sat Orm. The king had not taken his eyes off his brother as Arthur took in the sheer majesty the throne room presented.

Arthur was about to speak when two figures rounded the corner: Vulko, with Mera on his arm. His mentor was dressed in his purple robes lined with golden scales, the attire of a royal adviser. As Vulko led Mera past Orm, the king smiled at the princess, but his smile never reached his eyes. Mera was wearing the same green-scaled armor Arthur had met her in. Her hair was bound up and a golden tiara sat upon her head. A warrior and a princess to the core.

*The division between royalty and the rest of the population has never been clearer anywhere in the world, surface or below,* Arthur thought. This was what his two allies who now flanked Orm wanted him to become? Arthur vowed never to parade himself like that.

Orm stood.

"Brother." To Arthur's surprise, he saw that Orm was *smiling* at him. "I can't believe you're finally here. I've heard stories, all my life, of the son my mother bore with a surface dweller. A son who refused to acknowledge his other half, the Atlantean blood that runs through his veins. I was ashamed to have such a brother. Angered, even. But now that you're here, I have to admit . . ."

Orm's voice trailed off. He stared at Arthur for a moment before finishing his thought.

"I am conflicted."

Arthur lunged at him with a speed and force that nearly caught the guards unaware. They yanked his chains back just as he was inches from Orm's face. Orm didn't flinch.

Lips curled, Arthur looked upon his brother with nothing but hatred. "You want conflict? Unchain me and we'll see who's left standing!"

At Arthur's words, Orm's shoulders dropped slightly. Vulko couldn't help but notice. Neither could Arthur. Orm looked at the weapon one of the guards held.

"I see you brought our mother's trident. Is that why you came here at last? To challenge your own brother?" Though Orm tried to mask it with bravado, there was a stung tone to his voice.

"I came to stop a madman from destroying the world and getting us all killed," Arthur said flatly.

Orm straightened. "I see. And just how do you plan on

stopping the surface world from destroying us?" He began to walk around Arthur. As he spoke, the water shifted and glowed, holographic images forming, laying out the scenes he began to describe.

"For a century, they have polluted our waters." An oil spill from a broken tanker formed, then melded into speared whales. "Killed our children and those who dwell in harmony with us." The sea turned to fire around Arthur. "Now their skies burn and the oceans boil." The flames parted as Orm turned and leaned into Arthur. "*These* are who you side yourself with over your own kind?"

Arthur held his head up defiantly. "There are no sides in a war like this."

Orm scratched his cheek and sighed. "Arthur. Do you realize your mere presence here presents a challenge to my throne if you are not here to join me?"

"I'll do what it takes to stop your war." Arthur glared at his brother.

"Brother." Orm tsked. "I had wished this would turn out differently. I was prepared to offer for you to join us. But you're making it difficult."

"Good. I want no part of you." Arthur's words stung. "If getting you off that throne saves the world, then I'm down, 'brother.'"

At this, all hope Orm had of having a relationship disappeared, exiting his body in a sigh. In its place formed anger, and an idea.

"Are you invoking the 'Combat of the Kings,' then?" Orm said, a cold smile forming.

"Nice name. Sure, I invoke it. Bring it," Arthur shot back.

Orm rubbed his hands together. "Well, then that's how we shall proceed."

At his words, both Mera and Vulko stood in protest.

"Your Highness!" Vulko's voice warned.

"Orm, please. Don't—" Mera's plea was cut short.

Orm turned to them, addressing them as if they were children. "Don't you see? He leaves me with no other choice. Defeat the firstborn of Atlanna in a formal challenge, then everyone will have to concede. I will be named rightful ruler of the Seven Kingdoms."

"Your Majesty"—Mera's tone changed—"there is no honor in defeating the ignorant." Arthur's eyes turned to her at the perceived insult. Her eyes met his, seeming to say, *Play along, fool.*

"He clearly doesn't know our ways," Vulko agreed.

"Then he is about to get a lesson." Turning to Arthur, he asked, "Are you officially challenging me?"

"If that's what it takes, yeah. I officially challenge you

to kick your butt to the bottom of the sea." Arthur smiled through gritted teeth. "And when I win?"

Orm smiled and held out his arms. "Then I cease all plans of attack and you will have stopped a war. But if I win, all you love will be destroyed." He clapped his hands together suddenly to punctuate his point.

"It's on, little brother," Arthur said coldly.

Orm turned to the guards. "So be it. I have accepted the challenge. Prepare him for the Ring of Fire!"

Arthur's face contorted in confusion as the guards pulled him away. Ring of—what? As he passed Mera, he saw her face pale and wondered if he'd bitten off more than he could chew.

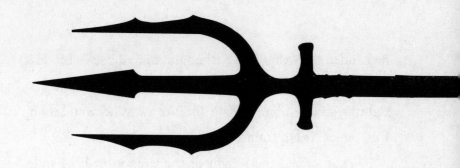

# EIGHT

The sun beat down on the beach in Amnesty Bay. A sixteen-year-old Arthur whipped his shaggy hair from his face, the tide's mist making it more of a mop than usual. Standing across from him, Vulko smiled as he saw Tom approach.

"I figured this day would come eventually," Tom said as he walked to the teacher and student.

Arthur looked at what his father was carrying. "Mother's trident?"

"Had to come off the wall eventually. If it's in anyone's hands, it should be yours." Tom smiled, pride in his eyes, as he handed the weapon to Arthur and moved back a bit. He had waited years to see if Arthur had inherited Atlanna's fighting abilities. From a safe distance away, he would soon find out as Vulko trained his son.

Arthur tested the weight of the weapon in his hand. It was lighter than he had imagined. In his sixteen years, never once had he taken it off the wall. It was like a monument to his mother, something even his curiosity must not cave in to. As he touched the prongs gently, one cut his finger, a pinprick of blood forming. It was still sharp, even after all these years.

Vulko raised his own weapon—a spear—and pointed it at Arthur. "We have practiced sparring with spears, but if you ever wish to become an Atlantean king, you must master the traditional weapon of one." Arthur had barely turned his attention back to his mentor when he saw Vulko spring to action. "Defend yourself!"

Instinctively, Arthur twisted his body and swung the trident down with both hands, knocking the spear away. The weapon sliced through the air with ease, almost as a natural extension of Arthur's arm. As Vulko stepped back to his starting position again, Arthur moved the trident to hold in just one hand. Master and student began sparring, working to full speed.

Vulko dodged and weaved as Arthur thrust the trident at him. When Arthur swung it again, Vulko bent backward to avoid the blow. He circled Arthur, the two moving as if in a dance. Arthur was getting the hang of it, and he knew it. He flashed a cocky grin as he crouched down, ready to disarm Vulko. His teacher, however, had a different thought in mind.

With a flick, Vulko's spear danced to the top of his wrist and began to twist around as he twitched his hand back and forth. The spear spun like a propeller around his wrist, picking up speed. Arthur was about to rush his mentor when the twirling spear sucked water from the sea, which Vulko was standing ankle-deep in, and gushed it out with a forceful blast that sent Arthur flying back.

"What was *that*?!" Arthur's eyes lit in amazement.

"A move I'll teach you when you have mastered the trident," Vulko said.

Looking at the rocks where his father had found Atlanna before he was born, Arthur slowly walked there, lost in thought. Dark thoughts he'd buried for years. He sat on the rocks and found Vulko had followed.

"This is my mother's trident, yeah? So why isn't she here teaching me how to use it instead of you?"

Vulko's tone was measured. "It is not the job of a queen—"

"It's the job of a mother!" Arthur yelled, pent-up anger finally rising to the surface. "Why has she never come to see me?"

"Son . . ." Tom reached his hand out to try and calm Arthur, but Vulko raised his own hand, signaling that he could handle this.

Vulko looked at the boy calmly. "As I have said, when you are ready—"

"*STOP LYING TO ME!*" Arthur yelled. "You've said this to me after every lesson. When will I be good enough for her? Or . . ." Arthur took a breath, speaking the words he had buried deep inside for years.

"Does she not love me?" His voice cracked. Tom turned away and walked back to his outpost on the pier, leaving Vulko to tell the tale he himself refused to believe.

Vulko softened. "Your mother loved you very much."

"Loved?" Arthur asked. Then as realization began to set in, he looked at Vulko, paling.

"She kept your birth a secret from King Orvax for years. But when he found out she'd had a son with a surface dweller, his jealousy took over." Vulko took a moment, dreading his next words. "He sacrificed her to the creatures of the Trench Kingdom, those that dwell where light cannot penetrate the darkness, and from which no Atlantean has ever returned."

Arthur began to shake as anger crashed through him like the high tide. Tears stung his eyes. "No. No, no, no," he muttered, his head bowed. Then, looking up slightly, his eyes grew ice-cold, staring at Vulko with a fury the man had never seen.

Even-toned, Arthur confronted his mentor. "They executed her? Are you saying they *killed* my mother? Murdered her because she had *me*?"

Vulko couldn't look Arthur in the eye. The boy suddenly turned and hurled the trident into the base of the pier, twenty feet away. Tom looked down at his son, heart in his throat. He refused to believe Atlanna was dead, and hoped one day Arthur would as well.

For the moment, Arthur had only anger in him. He turned to Vulko and shouted, "Never ask me to return with you into the sea. I want nothing to do with Atlantis!"

As Arthur walked away, Vulko prayed to Poseidon that the rightful heir to the throne would one day change his mind.

Vulko escorted Arthur from the Atlantean armory and headed for the Coliseum. Arthur was wider and taller than most Atlanteans, due to his mixed heritage, which meant the hand-me-down armor he'd found to put on was ill-fitting. Vulko, holding Atlanna's trident, stopped Arthur in the corridor, unable to hold his tongue any longer.

"How could you be so foolish? You let Orm bait you into a fight," Vulko whispered harshly.

Arthur gave him a surprised look. "I thought you were supposed to be the royal adviser. You wouldn't have told me to do this? I just solved all our problems. I beat him in combat, war is over, I go home."

"No question, Arthur, that you are a formidable fighter on land—but you are out of your element here. Literally." Vulko waved his arm through the water that surrounded them. "Orm has spent his entire life underwater. Training to be a warrior. Training to be the best."

"You taught me how to fight. Worried you didn't do enough? Because now isn't the best time to bring that up," Arthur said, eyebrow raised.

Vulko sighed. His apprentice was as stubborn as ever. "You've become a strong fighter in your own right, Arthur, but Orm will offer you no quarter whatsoever. Two combatants enter the Ring of Fire. Only one emerges." He thrust Atlanna's trident into his former student's hand. "I pray it's you."

The words hung in the air between them before Arthur nodded his head and the pair made their way to the entrance of the Coliseum. They entered a sparring room where Orm and Mera stood, talking quietly. Arthur looked around, unimpressed, but then his eyes caught on Mera.

Her hair was swept up, revealing a dress with silver lace on top that flowed into soft blues and reds. It moved with the water like a jellyfish. Appropriate for the Xebellian woman: a beautiful and deadly creature.

"You look radiant," Orm was saying.

Mera looked across the room to Arthur, her expression unreadable, before turning forcefully to face Orm. She gave only a nod in answer.

Orm reached into a pocket of his robe and pulled out a small bracelet. A precious stone inset in the center glimmered green in the light. He took Mera's hand.

"It matches your eyes." Orm smiled, a fond memory crossing his mind. "I have always thought you and my mother had similar eyes. Emerald and strong. It's fitting you have this, then."

Mera opened her mouth to object, but Orm raised her hand and kissed it before slipping the bracelet on her and said, "It belonged to my mother, our former queen."

Mera couldn't hold her tongue any longer. "Your mother . . . What would she think, seeing her sons fight like this?" she hissed, pulling her hand away. She gingerly fidgeted with the bracelet that now encircled her wrist.

Orm's blue eyes flashed, but he didn't take the bait.

Finally, Arthur broke the silence. "So this is the big 'Ring of Fire,' huh? How's this work? I kick your ass right here and now?"

Orm smiled at Vulko and Mera, neither of whom looked at Arthur, as if the three were coconspirators in a secret Arthur was left out of.

"Vulko," he said, waving Mera forward. "Will you please escort my fiancée to the royal box? It has the best view."

*Fiancée?* Arthur flashed Mera a look of confusion, but Mera just gazed coolly back at him. Alone, Arthur turned to Orm. Aware of the guards, Arthur got as close as he could to his brother, who was holding his shark-finned helmet in one hand and a wicked-looking trident in the other. Arthur held his own less ornate helmet and their mother's trident. A moment passed as the brothers seemed to size each other up.

"You know," Arthur said with a chuckle that surprised Orm, "there was a time when I wanted to meet you more than anything. Get to know my little brother. Let him know he wasn't alone. That we were in this together."

Arthur watched as a look of surprise crossed Orm's face. Had his brother wanted the same? Arthur brushed away the thought; any hope of reconciliation was long gone.

"If only I had known what a jerk you had turned out to be."

There was no reaction from Orm. Gone were the temper and bravado. Just a man—a madman, yes—who lifted his head to look at his brother one last time to admit something he had never said aloud before.

"I don't want to kill you, Arthur," he said. Arthur was shocked at the sincerity in Orm's voice. "I'm going to give you one last chance. Go home. Don't ever come back to Atlantis. You're not going to win this." Orm's voice changed from compassion to resilience. "A war is coming to the surface whether you like it or not, and I'm bringing the wrath of the Seven Seas with me."

Arthur steeled himself. "I can't let that happen."

"I know," Orm said regretfully.

Suddenly, the brothers' meeting was interrupted by the sound of a loud *BOOM* that sent vibrations through the water and rattled Arthur's teeth.

"What the hell is this?" Arthur asked.

Orm gave his brother a deadly grin. The time for talk had passed. "This? This is what you asked for."

The ceiling above suddenly split open and a hot red glow lit the room. Orm looked back at Arthur.

"The Ring of Fire!" he proclaimed as he launched himself out of the sparring room and through the opening. Arthur followed him through.

"Crap," he muttered. "You guys take this whole 'Ring of Fire' literally, don't you?"

The Coliseum was a massive structure built into the cone of an underwater volcano. The citizens of Atlantis were on their feet in the seating that stretched all the way around the rim. The *boom* noise Arthur had heard continued. He turned to see a massive octopus pounding the largest ceremonial drum Arthur had ever laid eyes on. The thumping of the drum was echoed by the stomping of hundreds of thousands of Atlanteans gathered to watch a once-in-a-lifetime duel.

Arthur looked around to take in the enormity of the

Coliseum. *The Romans had nothing on this*, he thought. Both majestic and brutal at once, the venue sported two large statues of ancient Atlantean warriors, swords held high. At each of their feet was a spout from which molten lava flowed. Scanning, Arthur saw other outcroppings that spurted lava as well. This was an *active* volcano, somehow kept in check by Atlantean technology!

The statues flanked the royal box, where Arthur saw Vulko nervously fidgeting with his robes as he met Arthur's gaze. Seated near him was Mera. Next to her was a behemoth of a man in segmented armor that reminded Arthur of Mera's ship. The crown on his head confirmed Arthur's suspicions: this must be Xebel's king, Mera's father, Nereus.

Turning his attention back to the Coliseum, Arthur noticed a round pedestal in the center of the volcano, built on volcanic rock and shaped into a perfect circle, rising from depths unknown and surrounded by spouts that shot out lava intermittently.

*The Ring of Fire*, Arthur had to admit, was nothing if not properly named. And it was possibly the most appropriate place for a challenge of kings, or whatever Orm had called it.

He barely had time to swim to the pedestal and take his place before his brother addressed his subjects, all of whom let out a mighty roar. Orm raised his trident, and the Coliseum fell deathly silent.

"People of Atlantis, hear me!" Orm cried, his voice filling the venue. "My brother has come from the surface to challenge me for the throne. Let us settle his claim in the ancient way! By bloodshed do the gods make known their will!"

Orm pointed his trident at Arthur. The Coliseum filled with the sound of boos. Arthur hadn't expected a warm welcome.

In the royal box, Mera turned to her father, her face unable to hide her disgust. "I never thought I'd see the day my own father bowed before the King of Atlantis," she spat.

Nereus sat up taller, meeting her gaze with a stern look. "I have not bowed to him," he corrected his daughter. "But I will stand with him. For now."

Mera was perplexed. "I agreed to marry him to prevent wars, not start one."

"The surface dwellers drew first blood. What would you have us do? Beg for mercy?"

Mera looked at him curiously. "The timing of that seemed a bit convenient, don't you think?" Her father did not answer. Realization dawned on Mera. "No. You wouldn't be that gullible. You want this, *too.*"

Nereus spoke, his gazed fixed on Arthur and Orm. "It is time the surface dwellers knew their place in the world. If this is how it must be done, so be it."

Mera's skin crawled. Suddenly, she felt as alone in this world as Arthur. She looked away from her father, no longer recognizable to her, and faced the center of the ring, offering up a silent prayer for Arthur's safety in the coming duel.

A loud blaring sound came from a giant conch shell, signaling the combatants to take their places. The brothers faced each other and tapped their tridents together in ceremonial greeting.

"You have our mother's trident. Powerful. But flawed. Like her," Orm said, looking upon his rival. His voice chilled. "I wield my father's, which has never known defeat!"

He lunged at his brother, striking suddenly. Catching Arthur off guard, the trident found a bit of exposed flesh on Arthur's arm and drew first blood as Arthur tried to parry. Orm raised his trident and swung it down toward Arthur's head. The other man barely had time to block as the two tridents clashed. The blow knocked Arthur back in shock. Orm *had* trained for this. And underwater, he was stronger.

Mera squirmed in her seat as she watched the battle. Arthur was not prepared for this, so she would have to come up with an alternative, just in case.

The brothers sparred, clashing tridents and getting in close enough to deliver blows with their fists. Soon, both were covered in slices and signs of bruising. Their clashing took them higher and higher until they were eye level with the crowd, which was riotous in its cheering.

Mera, seeing the battle clearly lopsided, stole a glance at her father. He was watching the battle of brothers unfold unblinkingly. Silently, she rose from her seat and swam back into the corridor behind them. She needed to act now.

With a swift twist, Orm angled his arm past Arthur's defenses and snared his brother in a headlock. Without missing a beat, Orm used the momentum to drive Arthur down, heading for the pouring lava beneath.

"Bow before me in front of all of Atlantis, and I will let you live out your remaining days in prison," Orm said as he dived. The water was getting hotter as they approached the lava. Orm continued the dive, aiming Arthur's head toward the molten flames.

"Or die in the Ring of Fire!" Orm's cry prompted a deafening roar from the crowd.

Arthur flexed, renewed fight flowing through him. He broke free of Orm's grasp and flipped his brother over his head, nearly shoving the king into the lava meant for Arthur's head. He swiftly jetted to the platform only to see Orm scoop the lava with his trident and hurl it at Arthur. It quickly hardened as it arced through the water, forming into a dense rock aimed directly at Arthur's head. Arthur swung his trident down and split the rock in two. He swung the trident back up without looking, anticipating his brother's next move. The trident hit Orm, glancing off his helmet. Orm knelt and the crowd gasped. Suddenly, who would be the victor was not so clear-cut.

Arthur began to twirl his trident around his arm, having mastered the move years ago. But to his surprise, the propeller motion began to waffle. Vulko had warned him he was out of his element. Arthur hadn't attempted this move underwater and didn't anticipate the resistance it brought.

Seeing his brother falter, Orm caught his opening. He swung his father's trident down with a furious cry. It connected with their mother's trident in a clash so powerful it drove both men back. Orm was quick to recover and sprung forward, attacking over and over. Arthur scrambled to parry each blow. Then, to Arthur's horror, the prongs of his trident began to crack. He let go of the weapon just as it shattered in half. Before he could recover, Orm kicked him in the chest, dealing a crippling blow that knocked Arthur on his back, crashing into the platform.

The crowd began to chant in unison: "KILL HIM! KILL HIM!"

Spurred on by the audience's bloodlust, Orm raised his trident high above his head. In the royal box, Vulko paled.

"I am the one *true* king of Atlantis!" Orm said, face twisted in rage.

Before he could deliver the killing blow, Orm found himself at the center of a growing vortex as the water around him churned. Suddenly, where Orm had once been floating in water, he found himself crashing to the base of the platform as the water emptied around him. The water vortex turned in on itself and pummeled wave upon wave at Orm, pressing him off the platform and driving him down into the depths below. Arthur realized only one person could be responsible for such a show of hydrokinesis.

Arthu looked up, and his suspicions were confirmed. There, in her armored ship floating above him, was Mera.

The canopy of the cockpit dissolved away as Mera, dressed once more in her green battle armor, motioned for Arthur to join her. "Waiting for a formal invitation?"

Arthur jetted to her, climbing in and taking a seat next to her. "Thanks," he breathed.

In the royal box below, Nereus looked aghast at his daughter's betrayal. The crowed erupted in boos, crying foul. Vulko seemed the only person showing a sign of relief. From the center of the Ring of Fire, Orm let out a furious cry.

"MERA!"

But the ship had already taken off.

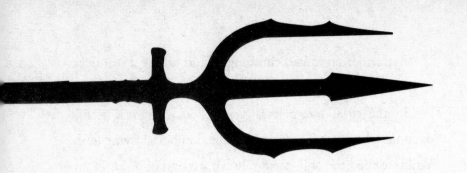

# NINE

"So, what's the plan?" Arthur was bandaging his arm in the cockpit.

"Some smaller cuts and scrapes are already mending thanks to your Atlantean blood. However, we need to get you somewhere safe so your body can fully heal." *As well as your pride*, Mera did not say. "If only you had followed the plan!" she blurted out.

"Which was?"

"Get to Atlan's trident and *then* challenge Orm!" She was exasperated, but silently relieved he was away from the Ring of Fire.

"So we're doing things a little out of order. Things happen!" Arthur caught a glimpse from the corner of his eye: an Atlantean guard ship. "We got a bogey on our six."

Mera looked sharply at him as if he was speaking a different language. He motioned behind them.

"Bad guy behind you."

Mera flung her controls hard, turning to narrowly evade a missile the ship had fired at them. "Then just say that!"

As the ship tilted, a cylinder slipped from the pouch at Mera's side. Arthur grabbed it and immediately recognized it—Vulko had shown it to them in the safe house. This was the first time Arthur had a chance to examine it closely.

"You're going after the trident?!" he exclaimed.

"Someone has to," Mera fired back as she made another evasive maneuver.

Arthur held on to the cylinder, arms folded. "Well, you'll need my help."

"*Your* help? *I'm* the one who just saved *you*!"

As he opened his mouth to protest, Arthur realized they were headed straight for the wall surrounding Atlantis rather than Gateway Bridge.

"Wait, I thought you said we can't go over these walls . . . ," he said, his voice trailing off.

Mera nodded, focused on what was ahead. "I did."

"You said there were hydro-cannons!" Arthur began to panic.

"I did!" Mera's ship surged forward, heading directly for one of the cannons.

Before the cannon could fire, a royal craft rose behind them and a volley of missiles sped toward their craft. One missile hit the ship's stern, blasting it apart. Mera struggled to steer over the wall.

"We're not dead yet," she said, bracing herself. She pressed a button as the ship careened end over end past the wall. Grabbing Arthur, she pulled the two of them out of the cockpit, ejectors giving them added momentum. *Much-needed momentum*, Arthur thought, as the ship exploded feet from them. The blast knocked them into the mountainside that bordered Atlantis's wall.

Catching their breath, Arthur and Mera stared at each other. "Now, hopefully they think we *are* dead," Mera said simply.

"This was your plan?!" Arthur looked at her in shock.

In the royal craft, Orm watched Mera's ship tumble into the depths beyond the wall, showing no sign of life. His stomach dropped, knowing he had possibly killed his fiancée and brother. He cursed as he steered his vessel back to the palace, a feeling deep within him that the pair had somehow escaped. He passed a pod of blue whales as he reentered the city.

"My turn," Arthur said, turning toward the approaching whales. One broke away from the rest and made its way to the duo. It dwarfed Mera and Arthur, but Arthur was unfazed. In fact, Arthur gently touched the whale, like an old friend. The whale opened her mouth. Arthur turned, seeing Mera staring in disbelief.

"What are you doing?" she breathed.

"Hop in." Arthur smiled back at her. "It worked for Pinocchio."

Mera was utterly lost at the reference. Her eyes widened as they began to move into the whale's open jaw.

"Oh, good, we're being eaten."

Arthur took her hand. She didn't pull it away. "Just relax, will ya? I'm pretty sure she doesn't think we're food."

Mera looked at him in disbelief. "How can I trust you? Or this whale the size of your ego?"

"Um, because I'm *saving* you!" Arthur was indignant as the whale began to close her mouth.

"I saved you first," Mera retorted.

"As long as we're keeping score . . ." Arthur lifted the

golden canister. "I'm ready to save us twice." He ran his fingers over the glyphs scrawled across the cylinder. "See these markings? These look like people, and they're surrounding this opening—which looks like a keyhole to me. And I think *this* is supposed to look like some kind of city—but there are currents of water running through it." Arthur broke into a grin. "Like a half-sunken city."

"What are you smiling at?" Mera asked.

"I love Venice this time of year."

In the royal palace, Orm paced furiously as Nereus sat, all color drained from his face at the thought of his daughter's death. Vulko stood in the corner, caught in a delicate balance of maintaining an appearance of loyalty without betraying his true nervousness for Mera and Arthur. Murk entered the room.

"We've located them, Your Highness," he said, holding up a holoprojector. It showed a blue dot moving through the waters.

"She lives?" Nereus rose suddenly.

"Apparently, I was mistaken," Orm said. "Dispatch all forces. Arrest them and make sure the princess is returned unharmed."

Murk nodded. "I shall send out *everyone* we have at our

service to aid." He and Orm exchanged a knowing look. Vulko realized suddenly that the two men shared a secret.

As Murk swam away and Orm and Nereus reviewed all paths the fugitives could have taken, Vulko's stomach dropped. Something was coming for his friends. And for once, he had no idea what it was. And worse, no idea how to warn them.

The sleek navy ship that David now called home was docked on an abandoned island far off any shore, in international waters. The waters lapped at its side. Suddenly, David broke through the surface of the water, holding a spear, his dinner on the receiving end. He had been practicing his deep-sea diving and hunting skills in the weeks since he had last seen the Atlantean named Murk.

David climbed ashore and started a small fire, preparing to cook his meal. He stiffened as he heard footsteps hitting the water. Without turning, he addressed the figure. "You're back."

Murk approached him, flanked by three armored guards. In their hands they held a large chest, which they dropped at David's feet before they moved behind their commander. "We have unfinished business," said Murk.

Murk took out the holoprojector, and Orm's face

appeared in the water that floated above it.

"Thought we were through." David remembered the last time he made a deal with the Atlantean king, and it hadn't gone his way.

"And I thought you wanted to kill Aquaman," came Orm's voice.

David unfolded his arms as Murk opened the case, revealing sleek white armor, similar to the kind the Atlantean guards in front of him were wearing, but different. Having pirated his fair share of ships, David knew an upgrade when he saw it, and this was definitely next generation.

"What's this?" David asked.

"Everything you need." Orm's voice was confident. "He defeated you last time because your surface weapons failed you. Ours won't." David could hear the disdain in Orm's voice at the word "surface," but he didn't care.

Murk nodded at the armor and its accompanying weapons. "Projectile resistant, strength-enhancing exo-skeleton. Underwater jet pack. Hydro-cannon. Sword is Atlantean steel."

David was impressed. He lifted the helmet and put it on. Instantly, the screen lit up, showing him navigational charts, system status updates, and a rearview display. He saw a blue dot appear on-screen. It was moving toward the familiar outline of Italy's coast.

Taking off the helmet, David turned back to Orm. "Nice rig. White's not exactly my color, though. May have to change that."

"Do what you will, but you are now responsible for leading these four of my finest commandos to hunt down and kill the half-breed abomination," Orm said. "Upon completion, you will be rewarded."

"Killing Aquaman *is* my reward." David picked up the suit, nodded in agreement to Orm's holo-head, and boarded his sub.

Orm's attention shifted to Murk. "How do you have such faith in this surface dweller?" Orm wasn't convinced.

"Because, like you, my king, he is motivated." Murk gave a confident smile. "More important, he smells blood in the water."

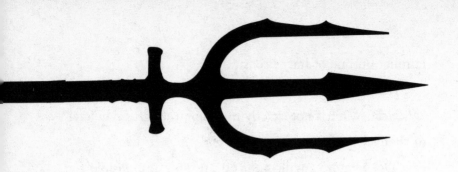

# TEN

"Ah, Venice. Just enough water-to-building ratio that I feel at home." Arthur was stretching in the early morning sunlight, wearing a loose shirt and baggy pants cinched at the waist. "Have you ever had gelato for breakfast?"

He turned to Mera, who was fussing with the long white dress they had recently "acquired" for her. Arthur helped her with her overcoat and explained the clothes were necessary, as they would apparently attract the attention of the surface dwellers if the pair strolled through the streets in their armored suits.

"Gelato?" she asked, barely paying attention.

"Yeah. Like ice cream, but, uh, softer." Arthur hadn't stopped to think what an Atlantean—or Xebellian, in her case—diet would consist of.

"I have no idea what you are talking about," she said, although anything for breakfast sounded good to her, as she noticed an empty feeling in her stomach. She couldn't remember the last time she had eaten.

"It's best if I just show you." Arthur smiled at her. She could sense his ease now that he was back on dry land. "You'll love Venice. And don't worry. We'll find the trident and get you back home in no time. Trust me."

Mera looked at the waters of the canal, these waters that flowed into the sea, and suddenly felt all alone. She shook her head at Arthur. "I can't ever go back. I betrayed everything when I saved you."

Arthur was confused. "But you're engaged to the king. They have to take you back."

"The king, your brother, who nearly *killed* us when we fled?" She gave Arthur a sad look. "Atlantis is many things, but forgiving it is not. Even to royalty. Your mother came back and, well . . ." Her words hung in the air a moment.

She finally sighed. "If I returned now, I, too, would be sacrificed to the Trench."

Arthur's face darkened briefly at the mention of his mother's fate. Trying to shake it off, he forced a smile. "Now you don't have to marry a jerk you're not in love with, right?"

Mera's eyes didn't meet his. "My obligation was not of love. It was to my family and my nation, both of whom I have now turned my back on."

It suddenly dawned on Arthur that she was now as alone in this world as he had felt. Except he still had a home and a father he could return to. She'd risked everything to save him, not because of an obligation, but because she believed in him. He promised himself that her sacrifice would not be in vain.

He reached out to take Mera's hand and she gave it to him. He led her into the heart of the thriving Italian city that was coming to life for the day around them. *If she can't go home, maybe she can find some of the same joys I have on the surface*, Arthur thought as the two entered the Piazza San Marco. The massive square had been called the "drawing room of Europe," meaning it was a place welcome to all who wanted to sit and enjoy conversation, religion, and politics in one place. And food, of course. With its large Italian domes and gilded windows, St. Mark's Basilica dominated one whole wall of the square. A large bell tower was opposite, its clock nearing seven. A row of nearly a hundred stalls lined the square opposite St. Mark's, each awaiting a vendor to sell his or her goods.

It was just early enough that Mera and Arthur were able to witness this magnificent jewel of Venice as it shone and came to life.

The bell of the magnificent church rang out seven times. Mera's eyes grew wide in amazement as hundreds of pigeons lifted off the ground, flew in circles, and landed again in the piazza, among the dozens of tables and chairs that filled the area.

The piazza vendors were rolling out their umbrellas and stocking their carts with freshly baked sweets and breads. Butchers hung fresh meats; florists put out newly cut bouquets in a myriad of colors. Nearly a hundred people began to mill about, finding chairs to sit in and read the paper, or on their way to Mass at the adjacent cathedral. Whenever Arthur visited Venice, the beauty almost moved him to tears. Looking at Mera, he knew she was feeling the same.

"For someone who believes surface dwellers are barbaric and ignorant creatures, is this changing your mind a bit? I hope so," Arthur teased.

Mera felt a tug at the hem of her dress. Looking down, she saw a little girl who gave an embarrassed giggle. Mera knelt beside the girl, who said something in a language Mera didn't understand, but Mera smiled anyway.

"She said she thinks you're very pretty and she likes your dress," Arthur translated.

Mera looked at him, trying to hide how impressed she was. He spoke multiple languages, obviously, but there was more. Arthur truly was a person of this world. All of it, not just his own people. She realized just how deeply he cared for and would fight for the entire surface world, from a leader to the little girl who'd complimented her.

"How do I tell her 'thank you' and that she is beautiful also?" Mera asked.

Arthur told her the words in Italian, and Mera repeated the foreign tongue to the girl. "*Grazie, bella ragazza,*" Mera said.

The little girl pulled Mera away to a small fountain, leaving Arthur to examine the cylinder that had directed them there. Pulling out a coin, the girl kissed it and tossed it into the fountain.

"*Una* . . . 'wish,'" she said, looking at Mera with wide eyes.

Mera circled her finger and caused the water in the fountain to swirl. Suddenly, the water formed a seahorse, the girl's coin in its mouth!

"A wish for you," Mera said, smiling.

The little girl's eyes were as big as saucers. She held up a finger and ran to her mother. Rummaging through her mother's bag, she grabbed a book and returned to Mera, handing it to her. Mera tried to protest, but the girl insisted. It was hard to say no with a language barrier . . . and to such an adorable girl.

Mera turned and walked back to Arthur, flipping through the pages of the book.

"People are going to think you like these surface dwellers," Arthur said, a small grin on his face.

Mera cocked her head. "It would be very wrong to judge a place I haven't seen."

*Touché*, thought Arthur. He certainly had misjudged at least one thing. For once, he was happy to be corrected.

"Wait!" Mera's tone made Arthur reconsider his previous thought. "This book . . . *Pinocchio*? He's not even a real person?!"

"Soooo, how about that gelato? Hungry?" he asked, quickly changing the subject.

"Quite," she snapped.

As the two strode across the piazza to the gelato vendor set up near the far end of the canal, Arthur looked around. "So, the markings on the canister showed us a half-sunken city. Here we are. Now to find the keyhole." He tilted his head, looking at the architecture of St. Mark's Basilica. People crowded around the iconic building, just like the canister depicted. Mera turned to follow his gaze. "I think we have a match."

Wasting no time, the two crossed the piazza and brushed past the crowd, into the church.

The inside of the basilica was even more breathtaking than the exterior. The golden walls were adorned in paintings, and every surface seemed to glimmer with a different priceless object.

Mera took Arthur's arm and gestured toward a fountain made of solid gold.

"That's tenth century, at least," Arthur said as they walked to the front of the altar.

Mera waved her hand over the fountain like she had outside with the little girl. This time, however, her expression tightened with intense focus. She gasped slightly, and a key rose a few inches out of the water. Mera grasped it.

"You did it!" Arthur yelled, his voice echoing in the massive cathedral. He winced and glanced around to see if anyone had noticed them. The two made a beeline for the exit.

The piazza buzzed along with life, not noticing the odd couple cradling the key in their hands as they strode along the canal.

"Shall we open it?" Mera's hands were shaking.

Just then, a figure burst from the canal, rising high into the air and hurling a concussive grenade at them. It exploded just as Arthur grabbed Mera to shield her. The impact knocked the two back and caused a panic in the piazza as dozens of people ran for safety.

The figure marched through the clearing smoke. He wore a black suit, similar to the Atlantean guards, but sleeker somehow, and more menacing, Arthur thought. The helmet was certainly new, he noted, as a scrambled electronic voice tinged with malice and hatred issued forth.

"Loathsomeness waits and dreams in the deep, and

decay spreads over the tottering cities of men." The voice echoed through the piazza, sending more people screaming for shelter.

As the figure spoke, Murk and three Atlantean soldiers sprang from the water, each armed with hydro-cannons and lethal Atlantean steel swords. They fanned out, forming a semicircle that blocked Arthur and Mera from the canal.

Addressing the captain of the guard, Mera commanded, "I order you to stand down!" But the soldier didn't move. From behind, Murk made a chilling proclamation.

"Princess Mera. You have been charged with high treason." As she heard those words, it was clear the only way for her to ever see home again would be if Arthur were king.

Arthur instinctively placed his arm in front of Mera. "How did you find us—" he demanded.

"Your betrothed sends his best," the mysterious figure said to Mera, advancing closer.

Mera looked at her wrist. "The bracelet," she said, Orm's betrayal setting in. "He's been tracking us since the Ring of Fire!"

An earsplitting sound sliced through the air, and a massive blast of energy shot from the glowing red eyes in their enemy's helmet—hydro-plasma beams. The arc of energy struck Arthur squarely in the chest, sending him flying back. Mera darted after him.

"Hand me the key!" Arthur whispered, trying to catch his breath as she reached him. His shirt had been melted from his body from the blistering heat of the incredible weapon.

Mera shook her head. "The key and canister are safer with me!"

Arthur looked at her in disbelief. "Are we seriously arguing about this *now*?!" Mera gazed unflinchingly back at him. "Fine! New plan: keep the key and the canister separate. I won't let them get their hands on Atlan's trident."

Mera nodded, shoving the canister into his hands. She took off at a run across the piazza, drawing the soldiers and Murk into her wake.

Arthur scrambled to his feet as the man in the black suit grew closer. He felt strange, weakened, from the power of those plasma beams. "Who the hell *are* you?!" Arthur had never faced such a foe before.

"Maybe this will jog your memory," came the electronically scrambled voice, as he unsheathed his sword. He then raised his other hand and pointed it at Arthur.

A short blade sprang from his forearm. "'Let's not make a habit of it' were your words the last time we faced each other, right?"

Recognition hit Arthur like a tidal wave. "The guy from that Russian sub?"

"Call me 'Black Manta,'" he said, lunging. Arthur blocked the sword blows with his armor bracers. "Did you think you could leave me there to die and forget me?"

Black Manta kicked Arthur's legs from under him, toppling him forward onto the ground. At that moment, Black Manta struck quickly, slicing into Arthur's back. Arthur yelled in pain—and surprise. This man had been easy to dispatch when they met on that submarine, but now . . . Arthur could feel from the slices on his back that his enemy had drawn blood.

Mera heard Arthur's cry from across the piazza. So did the soldiers and Murk, who she was battling. Mera took the moment of distraction to disarm the nearest soldier and kick him back. Spinning, she swung the blade up at Murk and sliced clean through his hydro-cannon. She slammed the hilt of the blade into his face and then ran up his body, flipping over him!

She landed and spun around, ready to face the captain of the Atlantean guard, but was too late—the guard turned the hydro-cannon to her and blasted her right into the canal. She sank, her dress floating to the surface a few moments later.

Arthur's vision was going fuzzy from the pain, but he managed to land a blow. Black Manta saw Arthur leap into the air and land on a nearby rooftop. He followed him. The two men grappled until Black Manta managed to pull out a grenade. He pushed it against Arthur's thigh and stabbed through the O-ring of the pin and twisted it. He jammed the O-ring on the blade, trapping the grenade against him. Pain coursed up Arthur's body.

Black Manta leaned in. "This is how you left my father to die." He disengaged the blade from his forearm, leaving it lodged in Arthur's leg. Arthur gasped in pain. "Tides always turn if you're patient enough. Time to die, fish man."

With that, he kicked Arthur from the roof. The big man landed on the ground of the piazza, grenade still stuck. He was trapped—if he pulled the blade out, the grenade would blow him up, along with half the piazza. But if he stayed, Black Manta would surely kill him.

Worse, he realized as he looked around—Mera was nowhere to be seen.

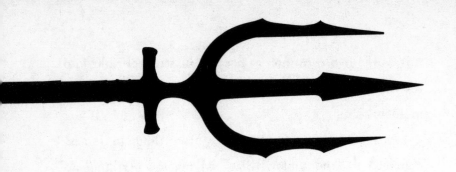

# *ELEVEN*

rthur was slow to get to his feet. As he pulled himself up, carefully holding the blade to not jostle the grenade, he called out to warn the few remaining people in the piazza to clear out.

"Aquaman'll save *their* lives? But you don't offer the same when someone begs you to save their father," Manta spat.

Arthur noticed from his vantage point that a glowing red light was climbing up the power pack on Black Manta's suit, like a loading bar. It looked like that horrible weapon was almost finished charging.

Gathering all his strength, Arthur grabbed a nearby

table and turned in time for the table to catch the brunt of the force of the plasma beam that shot from Black Manta's helmet. He flew across the square, crashing into tables and onto his back on the ground.

As Arthur struggled for air, he heard a familiar sound coming from the nearby canal. The water was churning. Black Manta was moving in for the kill, only to find that Arthur was painfully chuckling.

"You find death funny?"

"No," Arthur said, pointing at something behind Black Manta. "But gonna laugh my ass off when *she* gets through with you!"

Black Manta turned to see a magnificent sight. Mera, rising from the canal water, standing on the funnel she had created, emerald armor shining in the sun, her eyes glowing an electric blue.

"You fools thought you could drown me?" Her voice boomed across the piazza. "I command the water!"

With that, she threw her arms forward. Spears made of water struck the commandos, Murk, and Black Manta simultaneously, battering them far across the piazza, buying the duo a little time.

She rushed to Arthur, seeing the knife in his leg. "Look what I caught." Arthur chuckled. "Or, I guess it caught me."

Mera reached to remove the blade, but Arthur stopped her, pointing to the pin. Mera's eyes grew wide. There wasn't much time to devise a plan. Their enemies were already beginning to pull themselves together across the makeshift battlefield.

"Do you trust me?" Mera looked confidently at Arthur.

"You saved my life before, so why not?" Arthur smiled.

She motioned and water from the canal rose and jetted to her, floating in midair. She closed her eyes to concentrate, and the water began to swirl around them. It formed a mini-cyclone. A tiny bead of sweat formed on her brow, and the droplet lifted off her face to join the whirling mass that rose above them. The water swept through the air and settled onto Arthur's leg.

Arthur watched the mouth of the swirl tighten until it became a funnel. Suddenly, the blade slid from his body, pulling with it the grenade's pin. Before Arthur could protest, the grenade was caught up in the storm as well.

The water rose higher and higher, carrying with it the deadly explosive. When the water reached its apex, it formed a sphere around the grenade just as the metal ball exploded. The sound rocked the piazza, but nothing was damaged. Water from the explosion rained down across the square.

Mera opened her eyes and looked down at him. "I think we're even on saving each other," he said.

Mera smiled. "I'd agree," she whispered, parting her lips slightly as she looked down into his golden eyes.

Arthur's heart was pounding. *Must be the adrenaline*, he thought. Then, seeing the enemies approach behind them, he scrambled away from Mera and to his feet. "Hold that thought," he said.

Black Manta approached, his hydro-cannon spouting round after round into Arthur's chest.

"We played this game before, and you lost." Arthur sneered.

He reached out and grabbed the weapon in his hand. With a grunt, Arthur bent the barrel of the hydro-cannon up at a ninety-degree angle and wrenched it from Black Manta's hands. Anger flashed in Arthur's eyes. Quietly, he uttered, "My turn," and delivered a brutal uppercut to Black Manta, cracking the helmet and sending the man soaring backward.

For her part, Mera raised her arm and willed the water to cease, forming a wall in front of her. She gave a mighty heave, and the wall of water flew back at the men firing on her, knocking them to the ground.

She jumped, landing in front of Murk, and summoned

a thin tendril of water to her from the canal. She glowered at Murk and hissed, "You swore allegiance to the wrong king."

With that, the water tendril became a whip and snared Murk around the throat. It slammed him down, obeying the motions of Mera's arms. She hydrokinetically lifted him and flung him back to the sea.

Behind her, Arthur lunged for Black Manta. He saw the beams energize in the broken helmet's eyes and dodged as the blast exploded in multiple directions. David was caught as his blast backfired and he screamed in pain. The helmet shattered from his head.

His arm was pulled up by a woman's hand. Mera was on him! She slid the bracelet on his arm as she leaned in close. "Here. Let my 'betrothed' track you in the darkest depths."

She moved aside as Arthur pounced. He lifted Black Manta and ran with the man held over his head. He leapt over the canal and turned toward the sea that it spilled into.

Arthur looked up at David, bruised and bleeding. "Like I said," Arthur repeated, "let's not make a habit of this."

Mera's arms were raised, and the sea churned and spun, far from the boats in the harbor. Arthur leapt in the air and hurled David into the center of the whirlwind.

The sea swiftly dragged Black Manta down.

Mera lowered her arms. The waters calmed. The pair stood for a moment in the sudden silence before turning to each other.

Arthur shook his head slightly and brushed back his long wavy hair. His eyes grew serious. "That will buy us some time, but we need to leave. Now. Where the hell are we going?"

Mera held up the key. "I guess it's time to find out."

Arthur handed the golden canister to Mera, who inserted the key.

The container opened to reveal an ancient parchment, strange script scrawled across it. He stared at it hard, and then shook his head, handing it to Mera. "I can't read this."

Mera's lips curled into a rare grin. "Why? Is it in English?" Mera glanced at the page and her eyes widened. "*You* may not be able to read this, but I can!"

Arthur could barely contain the excitement in his voice. "Well?"

"The ancient ones smile on us. The trident of Atlan is not far, and the seas favor us, Arthur Curry," Mera said. Without another word, and trusting that he would follow, she turned to the water and dived straight in.

Arthur smiled. He couldn't believe he was following

a warrior princess back into the depths of the sea, chasing a trident of legend. And when they found it . . . Arthur was surprised that he suddenly felt worthy of it, worthy to be king.

With a giant leap, Arthur dived into the water after her, ready to claim his birthright . . . and with it, the throne of Atlantis.